...is lived in Belfast till the age of twelve. Leaving school at fifteen, he spent three years with the Royal Horse Guards, serving on the East German border during the Cold War. His subsequent employment included occupations as diverse as circus roustabout, truck driver, clerk and, after taking an honours degree in sociology and social psychology, teacher and university lecturer.

The Eagle Has Landed turned him into an international bestselling author, and his novels have since sold over 250 million copies and have been translated into sixty languages. In addition to *The Eagle Has Landed*, ten of them have been made into successful films. His recent novels include *The Wolf at the Door*, *The Judas Gate*, *A Devil is Waiting* and *The Death Trade*, which were all *Sunday Times* bestsellers.

In 1995 Jack Higgins was awarded an honorary doctorate by Leeds Metropolitan University. He is a fellow of the Royal Society of Arts and an expert scuba diver and marksman. In 2014 he was awarded an Honorary Doctorate of Literature by the University of London. He lives on Jersey.

JACK HIGGINS

Bad Company

HARPER

Harper
An imprint of
HarperCollins*Publishers*
1 London Bridge Street,
London SE1 9GF

www.harpercollins.co.uk

This paperback edition 2015

First published in Great Britain by HarperCollins*Publishers* 2003

Copyright © Harry Patterson 2003

Jack Higgins asserts the moral right to
be identified as the author of this work

A catalogue record for this book is
available from the British Library

ISBN: 978-0-00-812492-2

Set in Sabon by Born Group using Atomik ePublisher from Easypress

Printed by CPI Group (UK) Ltd, Croydon, CR0 4YY

MIX
Paper from
responsible sources
FSC
www.fsc.org
FSC® C007454

FSC is a non-profit international organization established
to promote the responsible management of the world's forests.
Products carrying the FSC label are independently certified
to assure consumers that they come from forests that are managed
to meet the social, economic and ecological needs
of present and future generations.

Find out more about HarperCollins and the environment at
www.harpercollins.co.uk/green

For Amber

DAUNCEY VILLAGE
WEST SUSSEX
2002

1

It was raining when they buried Kate Rashid, Countess of Loch Dhu, a rain that swept in across Dauncey Village like a solid curtain, sending people hurrying for the shelter of the church. They were all there, the great and the good, to say farewell, their cars blocking the High Street.

General Charles Ferguson's Daimler had just arrived. He sat there in the rear with Sean Dillon, who took a silver flask from his inside pocket, swallowed a little Bushmills whiskey and lit a cigarette.

'Are we going in?'

'No,' Ferguson said.

'Then why are we here?'

'It's the civilized thing to do, Dillon. It's a great story, after all. The world's richest woman crashing into the sea off the English coast at the controls of her own plane. Her cousin Rupert mysteriously disappeared.' He leaned back. 'You couldn't improve on it if it was a made-for-television movie.'

Dillon took another swig from his flask. 'I've said it before, but it's the cold-blooded bastard you are, General.'

'Really? I thought that was you, Dillon.'

'All right. But I repeat: if we're not going in, what are we doing here?'

'Patience, Dillon. I'm waiting for someone.'

'And who might that be?'

'Well, for starters, a good friend of yours.' A Mercedes rolled in and braked behind them. 'And here he is.'

Blake Johnson emerged, ran through the rain and scrambled into the back of the Daimler.

'Great to see you, General.' He took Dillon's hand. 'And you, my fine Irish friend.'

'And where in the hell have you come from?' Dillon demanded.

'The White House, of course.'

Blake was in his early fifties, his hair still black, and an ex-Marine. He was also Director of the White House's General Affairs Department, though everyone who knew it – which wasn't many – just called it 'the Basement'. In actuality, it was the President's private hit squad, totally separate from the CIA, the FBI, the Secret Service, or any other governmental organization.

Dillon was intrigued. 'But what are you here for?'

Ferguson ignored him. 'Is it true? About the Baron?'

'Yep. Just announced. The President ordered me straight to you, General, and here I am.'

'And who's this Baron creature when he's at home?' said Dillon.

'You're about to find out,' Ferguson said.

A Rolls-Royce pulled in at the church gate. A uniformed chauffeur emerged, got an umbrella up, and opened the rear door. A young man in his early thirties emerged, a trench coat over his shoulders, hurried to the other door and waited.

The man who stepped out was very old, wore a black leather overcoat and slouch hat, and carried a silver-topped walking stick. The young man held the umbrella over him, offered his arm and they went up the path to the church.

'There he goes,' Blake said.

Dillon frowned. 'Who is he?'

4

'Baron Max von Berger,' Ferguson said. 'An exceedingly rich man. And – as Blake has just confirmed – none other than Kate Rashid's silent partner.'

'Rashid?' Dillon said. 'Just a minute. Are you saying Berger as in Berger International?'

'That's right.'

'But they're worth billions.'

'Exactly.'

'And they now have control of Rashid Investments?'

'Unfortunately so.'

'Well,' Dillon said, and paused. '*That* could be a problem.'

The rain hammered on the roof, organ music swelled from the church. Blake said, 'Why does it always rain at funerals?'

'It's the way Hollywood does it,' Dillon said. 'It's life imitating art. Who was the hard man?'

'The one escorting him?' Blake nodded. 'Interesting you should call him that.'

'It's the broken nose, Blake: I'd hate to see what was left of the man who did that to him.'

Ferguson joined in. 'The name is Marco Rossi. He studied economics and business at Yale, then joined the Italian Air Force and flew a Tornado in Bosnia. You'd have a lot in common with him, Dillon. He was shot down and had a very energetic time behind Serb lines. Very unreasonable people, the Serbs, but then you know that. His mother once worked for the Baron. She was born in Palermo and, yes, her uncle, one Tino Rossi, was Mafia in a very big way.'

Dillon said, 'So what's young Marco up to now?'

It was Blake who answered. 'Amongst other things, he's taking over all security operations for Rashid Investments worldwide. Don't kid yourself, Sean. This guy is good. He's not to be screwed with, even on the pavement.' He shrugged. 'I've even met him on the social circuit in Washington. He's charming and civilized, and the women love him.'

'Only don't push him the wrong way,' Ferguson said. 'When he was on the run behind the Serb lines in Bosnia, he killed at least four men, that we know of. He keeps an ivory Madonna in his pocket. When you press the button, the blade jumps out and shears right up under the chin.' Ferguson smiled thinly. 'Your kind of man, Dillon.'

'So if he's taken over all the security operations at Rashid Investments, that means that he can access everything the Rashids ever had on us in their computers.'

'Exactly,' Ferguson said. 'Including how you shot Kate Rashid's three brothers and interfered rather harshly in their oil operations in Hazar. And I do think he's going to find it more than a remarkable coincidence, that Kate Rashid subsequently went into the drink at the controls of her Black Eagle and her dear cousin Rupert vanished off the face of the earth.'

'So they're going to be coming for us.'

'Oh yes, Dillon. I should very much think so.'

He reached into his briefcase and extracted a large envelope.

'You'll want to read all of that. Especially the bit about what von Berger did in World War II. That's especially enlightening.'

He leaned back. 'Yes, Dillon, I think we're in for a very, *very* interesting time of it.'

BERLIN
THE FÜHRER BUNKER
30 APRIL 1945

2

If there was a hell on earth it was Berlin. It seemed to be on fire, a charnel house, black smoke drifting everywhere. The city was doomed, everyone knew that, and the Russians were already in control of the eastern half.

The people were on the move, refugees from their own city, carrying what they could, a few pitiful belongings, with the desperate hope that they might somehow get to the West and reach the advancing American army.

Groups of SS were stopping anyone in uniform. Those without a pass or some sort of order were shot on the spot. Shells were dropping in, fired at random by Russian artillery. People cried out in alarm and scattered.

Sturmbannführer Baron Max von Berger sat in the front passenger seat of a *Kubelwagen*, the German equivalent of a jeep. He had an SS corporal driving, a sergeant in the rear seat clutching an MP40 Schmeisser machine pistol. As they moved along the Wilhelmstrasse close to the Reich Chancellery, they saw three SS soldiers with two men in civilian clothes on their knees, about to be shot.

Von Berger told his driver to halt. 'Stop!' he said. 'What is your authority for this?'

The men paused. Their leader, a sergeant, had a brutal unshaven face. He took in von Berger's black leather coat and the young face, and failed to notice the Knight's Cross with Oak Leaves and Swords under the collar of the coat.

'And who the hell are you, sonny?'

'*Sturmbannführer* von Berger.'

The smell of brandy was powerful. 'At your age? You look about nineteen. I bet you stole the uniforms, you and your mates here.' He cocked his Schmeisser. 'Let's see *your* authority.'

'Oh, I can show you that.'

Max von Berger took a Luger from his right-hand coat pocket and shot him between the eyes. The sergeant in the rear of the *Kubelwagen* sprayed the other two as they turned to run.

The two men who had been faced with death got up in a daze and von Berger waved them away. 'Clear off.' He turned to his driver. 'Carry on.'

The *Kubelwagen* turned out of Wilhelmstrasse and into Vossstrasse and approached the Reich Chancellery, which was, like everything else, a victim of the bombardment, defaced and crumbling. It had long since passed functioning as any kind of headquarters, but under thirty metres of concrete was Adolf Hitler's last command post, the Führer Bunker. It was a self-supporting, subterranean world complete with electricity, fresh water and extensive kitchens; still in touch with the outside world by radio and telephone; and crowded with people like Bormann and Ribbentrop and numerous generals, all trying to avoid the harsh reality that thirty metres over their heads, the Third Reich was coming to a disastrous end.

The vehicle ramp was ruined, but there was room to park the *Kubelwagen* to one side. The SS sergeant got out and opened the door for von Berger. 'Quick thinking, Herr Baron.'

'A reflex, Karl – it's been a long war. You didn't do too badly yourself.' He got out, reached for a briefcase, turned and walked to the two SS sentries at the Bunker entrance.

They sprang to attention. '*Sturmbannführer.*'

'One of you deliver this to Major-General Mohnke's aide. It's the report the general wanted on the state of Number Two Brigade's readiness for the final assault.' One of the men took it and went downstairs. Von Berger turned to the other and clapped him on the shoulder. 'Find me a drink. I was shot in the left hip last year, and some mornings it hurts like the devil. I'll be in the garden.'

The boy went off at the double and von Berger said, 'Come on, Karl,' and went round to the once-lovely garden, now a wreck, with some trees uprooted, the occasional shell hole. There was a sadness to the place for what once had been and, for a moment, the artillery seemed like only the sound of distant thunder on the horizon. He took out a cigarette case, selected one, and Karl Hoffer gave him a light. A tough, hard young man of twenty-five, Hoffer was a forester from the Baron's great estate in the forest of Holstein Heath, the *Schwarze Platz*, the dark place. They'd served together for four years.

'So, my friend, we're in a fine fix, aren't we?'

'We were in Stalingrad, too, but we made it out, Baron.'

'Not this time, Karl. I'm afraid we might have to take up permanent residence. I wonder what it's like at home.'

He was thinking of Schloss Adler above the village of Neustadt. It had been his family home for seven hundred years, a huge expanse of forest, dark and mysterious, dotted with villages, every inhabitant a member of the extended family of which he was the head.

'Have you heard from the Baroness?' Hoffer asked.

'I had that letter four months ago, but nothing since. And you?'

'Just that one from my Lotte in February. She mentioned the Baroness, of course.' Lotte worked as her maid at the Schloss.

11

Von Berger's father, a major-general, had been killed during the Polish campaign in thirty-nine, elevating Max suddenly to the title of Baron. His mother had died at his birth. The only woman in his life was his beloved Elsa and they had married early because of the war. Like von Berger, she was twenty-three and the boy, little Otto, was three years of age.

The young SS guard appeared clutching a bottle and two glasses. 'I'm sorry, Herr Baron, it's vodka, I'm afraid.'

Max von Berger laughed. 'I'd say that's rather appropriate, but you've only brought two glasses.'

The boy flushed. 'Well, I did put one in my pocket, *Sturmbannführer*.'

The Baron turned to Hoffer. 'See how well we train them?' He took the bottle, jerked off the cork, then poured liberally into one of the glasses and tossed it down. He gasped, 'God, that hit the spot. The Russians made this one in the backyard.' He poured another, which went the same way. 'Great. Take that for a moment, Karl.'

'Baron.'

Von Berger removed his leather greatcoat and handed it to Hoffer. 'Suddenly my hip feels fine.' He poured a third vodka and gave the boy the bottle back. 'Now you two.'

He took a cigarette out of his case one-handed, the glass of vodka in the other. Hoffer gave him a light and the Baron walked away, enjoying his smoke and sipping the vodka.

Hoffer and the boy had a quick one and poured another. The boy was fascinated by von Berger. 'My God, his uniform. I've never seen anything like it.'

Hoffer was wearing combat camouflage gear. He shrugged. 'I've got the same thing under this lot. Except for the medals.' He grinned. 'The medals are all his.'

In spite of his youth, Baron Max von Berger had seen action in Poland, France and Holland with the Waffen SS. Afterwards, he'd transferred to the 21st SS Paratroop Battalion, and been wounded at Maleme in Crete. Then had come Rommel's Afrika Korps and the Winter War in Russia. He wore a gold badge, which meant he had been wounded five times.

Despite the silver Death's Head badge on his service cap and the SS runes and rank badges on his collar, he was all *Fallschirmjäger*, in flying blouse and jump trousers tucked into paratroop boots Luftwaffe-style, though in field grey.

The gold-and-silver eagle of the paratroopers' qualification was pinned to his left breast above the Iron Cross. The Knight's Cross with Oak Leaves and Swords hung from his throat.

Karl Hoffer said, 'He's special people, the Baron. We've been through four years of hell together and we're still here.'

'Maybe not for much longer,' the boy said.

'Who knows? In Stalingrad, we thought we'd had it, and then right at the end we both got wounded and they put us on one of the last planes out. Three hundred and fifty thousand men went down the drain, and we made it out.'

At that moment, General Mohnke appeared from the garden entrance of the Bunker. He ignored them and moved towards von Berger.

'Baron, the Führer wants to see you.'

Max von Berger turned, puzzlement on his face. 'The Führer?'

'Yes, at once.'

Von Berger paused beside Karl and held out his glass. Karl filled it and von Berger toasted him. 'To us, my friend, and the three hundred and sixty-five men of the battalion who died for whatever.' He tossed the drink back and threw the glass away. 'So, General,' he said to Mohnke, 'Let's not keep the Führer waiting.'

He followed the general down a flight of steps, the concrete walls damp with moisture. Soldiers, mainly SS, were crammed in every nook and cranny of the apparently endless

13

corridors and passageways. There was a general air of despair – more than that, resignation. When people talked, it was in subdued tones against the background of the whirring electric fans that controlled the ventilation system. The soldiers only stopped talking at the surprising sight of Max von Berger in his immaculately tailored uniform, medals aglow.

They passed through the lower levels that housed most of the Führer's personal staff, Goebbels and his family, Martin Bormann, and many generals. Mohnke still led the way, but von Berger knew exactly where he was going, for he had been there before.

In the garden bunker was the Führer's study, as well as a bedroom, two sitting rooms, bathroom facilities, and a map room, close by and convenient for the constant conferences. Mohnke knocked on the door and went in. Von Berger waited. There was a murmur of voices, then Mohnke returned.

'The Führer will see you now.' He grabbed the young man's hand. 'Your comrades of the SS are proud of you. Your victory is ours.'

A slogan initiated by Goebbels in one of his inspired moments, and the subject of much ribaldry in the ranks of the SS. In any case, von Berger couldn't imagine what he had done to cause such adulation.

'You're too kind, General.'

'Not at all.' Mohnke was sweating and looked slightly dazed. He stood back and von Berger passed into the study.

The Führer sat at his desk, leaning over a map. He seemed shrunken, the uniform jacket too large for him; the face seemed wasted, the eyes dark holes, no life there at all, his cheeks hollow, a man at the end of things. The young woman beside him was an SS auxiliary in uniform. She held a sheaf of documents, which she passed one by one for Hitler to

14

sign with a shaking hand. Her name was Sara Hesser. She was twenty-two years of age and had been pulled in by the Führer himself to act as a relief secretary.

He glanced up at her. 'Deliver these. I'll see the Baron in the sitting room. You can then bring the special file to me. Is it up to date?'

'As of last night, my Führer.'

'Good.' He stood up. 'Follow me, Baron.'

He shuffled ahead, opened the door and led the way into the first sitting room. He sat in an armchair by a coffee table.

'Baron Max von Berger, *Sturmbannführer* of the SS, you took a holy oath to protect your Führer. Repeat it now.'

Von Berger clicked his heels together. 'I will render unconditional obedience to the Führer of the German Reich and People, Adolf Hitler, Supreme Commander of the Armed Forces, and will be ready, as a brave soldier, to stake my life at any time on this oath.'

Hitler nodded in satisfaction. 'You have a magnificent record for one so young and yet you never joined the Nazi Party. Why not?'

'It didn't seem appropriate, my Führer.'

'A typical response from the head of a great family. The aristocrat to the end – and yet you served me well. Why was that?'

'It's a matter of honour, my Führer. I took the oath.'

'Just what I thought you'd say. You're a remarkable young man. I sensed that when I decorated you with the Swords. That's why I made you an aide. I was saving you. You'd be no use to me dead and that's what would have happened if you'd returned to the front.'

Max von Berger took a deep breath. 'What would you have me do, my Führer?'

'The most important task left to anyone in this Bunker. The Russians are coming. They want to cage me, and I can't

15

have that. My wife and I will commit suicide – no, no, don't look like that, von Berger. The important thing is my work must continue, and you will play a part in that, the most important part.'

By his wife, he was, of course, referring to his mistress, Eva Braun, whom he had married around midnight on the 28th.

'We must see that National Socialism survives, that is essential. We have vast sums of money, not only in Switzerland, but in South American countries sympathetic to our cause. Many of my emissaries are already in the Argentine and Brazil. We must maintain the *Kameradenwerk*, the Action for Comrades.'

There was a knock at the door and Sara Hesser came in, a briefcase in one hand. Hitler waved her to one side. 'I have no secrets from Sara, as you will see.'

'So where do I fit in, my Führer?'

Hitler raised a hand. 'The Führer Directive.'

Sara Hesser opened the briefcase, extracted a sheet of paper and passed it to von Berger, who read it with some astonishment. It was explicit:

The Führer Bunker, April 30, 1945.
The bearer of this pass, an aide on my staff, is
Sturmbannführer Baron Max von Berger, on a
personal assignment from me. All personnel, civil and
military, will render him every assistance.
Adolf Hitler

'This may help you,' Hitler said.

For Max von Berger, the implications were breathtaking. 'But in what way, my Führer?'

'To get through whatever happens to you in the next few days. To help you get home, to survive and prepare yourself for your inevitable capture by the Americans or British.'

16

Von Berger was bewildered. 'But there are no Americans here, my Führer, only Russians.'

'You don't understand. Listen. During the last few days, many planes have flown in from Gatow and Rechlin, using streets such as the East West Avenue near the Brandenburg Gate as runways. Field Marshal von Greim came in the other day in a Fieseler Storch.'

Max von Berger struggled to control himself. The only reason for von Greim to come to Berlin was to be promoted to head of the Luftwaffe. The Führer, of course, could have told him on the telephone. Instead, von Greim had flown in from Munich escorted by fifty fighters, and forty of them had been shot down.

He said patiently, 'And how does this affect me?'

'I spoke to the Commandant of the Luftwaffe base at Rechlin. A pilot has volunteered to fly you out in a Storch. It has already arrived and is waiting in that huge garage at Goebbels' house. The heavy rain and steam from the fires will make it an ideal time to go.'

'But to do what, my Führer?'

Hitler put out a shaking hand and Sara Hesser put the briefcase on the desk. 'When the war is over, industry will collapse and so will your family's company, Berger Steel. Eventually, though, things will start to improve, and especially for you. In here, you will find details of deposits in Switzerland, codewords, passwords, which will give you access to millions. You'll build Berger back into a power.'

Von Berger was speechless.

'That is not all.' Hitler opened the briefcase and produced a book bound in dark blue. 'I have kept a diary for the past six months, a time in which everyone has betrayed me. Goering, Himmler.' He shook his head. 'And no one tried more than me to be reasonable. I even sent Walter Schellenberg to Sweden to meet Roosevelt's representative, did you know

17

that? No, of course you didn't. I offered a negotiated peace to combat the Red menace. Am I the enemy? No. It is that dog Stalin. Together, the US and Germany, we could have smashed him, but, no, my offer was rejected. The Americans will reap the whirlwind, believe me. The Russians will not recognize what they have taken. The damage they will do to Berlin is beyond anyone's comprehension. Yet Roosevelt and Eisenhower have decided to hold back after the Elbe crossing. Patton and his tanks could be here in twenty-four hours, but they've been told to stay where they are, in obedience to Stalin's wishes, and allow the Reds to take Berlin.

'My God,' von Berger said.

'Believe me, in the years to come, America and Britain will rue this as their greatest folly. And it is all in my diary. Every day, I have dictated it to Fräulein Hesser. You may notice the trembling in my hand – an unfortunate ailment that has plagued me for some time. But I have signed each entry.'

'So what do I do with the diary, my Führer?'

'There will come a time when it will be of use to advance our cause. I do not know when – but you will, Baron. You will be its keeper. It is a holy book, Baron. I want no copies, your oath on that? Protected at all times. You may read it, if you wish. You will find the account of my dealings with Roosevelt particularly interesting.' He shook his head. 'I have every belief that you will achieve this for me.'

And Baron Max von Berger, a great soldier and a brave man, but who had always despised the Nazi Party, for some reason felt incredibly moved. The young woman put the diary and documents back into the briefcase and handed it to him.

Hitler said, 'So, you will leave within the next hour because of the bad weather.'

'May I take my sergeant with me?' von Berger asked.

'Of course. You can also take Fräulein Hesser.' He glanced up at her.

18

She said, 'No, my Führer, my place, my duty, is with you.'

'So be it.' Hitler stood and held a shaking hand to von Berger. 'Strange. Not even a Party member, and yet I chose you.'

Von Berger shook his hand strongly. 'I accept the task. It is a matter of honour.'

'On your way. We shall not meet again.'

Sara Hesser went and opened the door. Max von Berger, the briefcase in his hand, paused and turned, and the sight of Hitler, hunched at his desk, was to haunt him for his entire life.

'My Führer.' He gave a military salute.

Hitler gave a thin smile. 'Even now you cannot bring yourself to give me a Party salute. You touch your cap like a British Guards officer.'

'I'm sorry, my Führer.'

'Oh, go on. Just go.' Hitler waved his hand and Sara Hesser closed the door on the Baron.

He found his way back up the crowded passageways and through the garden Bunker, where he found Hoffer and the young SS soldier sitting under a concrete awning in the entrance, drinking the rest of the vodka while it rained relentlessly.

Hoffer stood up. 'Baron?'

'We're getting out, Karl. Believe it or not, but we're going to get out.'

'But how, sir?'

Von Berger took him to one side. 'I've been given a special mission by the Führer. There's a light plane waiting. I'm not saying more, but we're going home, we're going to Holstein.'

'I can't believe it.'

'Well, it's true. Give me my coat and get some weapons.'

He turned and the boy said, 'You're going, *Sturmbann-führer?*'

Von Berger smiled and clapped him on the shoulder. 'What's your name, boy?'

'Paul Schneider.'

'Then I'll tell you what, Paul Schneider. Instead of waiting to face death at the hands of the Russians, you can come with us, fly to the West, and surrender to the Americans.'

'I can't believe it,' the boy gasped.

'Sergeant Hoffer just said that.' He turned to Hoffer. 'Get moving.'

Within forty minutes, von Berger, Hoffer and young Schneider left the Bunker, exiting into Hermann Goering Strasse. They were well armed with military packs containing extra ammunition and grenades. Each one had a Schmeisser machine pistol slung across his chest.

There were people pouring along the Tiergarten in hordes now, a terrible panic having taken over, and the fog, made worse by the smoke, swirled across the city, not even the heavy rain managing to clear it. The rumble of artillery was constant, women with children screamed, terrified.

The three men moved along the Tiergarten on the edge of the crowd, cut across by the Brandenburg Gate to Goebbels' house. It showed evidence of damage, obviously from shell splinters, but the very large garage was intact. There was a Judas gate in the main door and Hoffer opened it gently.

'Hold it,' a voice called, and a light was switched on. A small Fieseler Storch spotter plane appeared, a young Luftwaffe captain standing beside it in uniform and flying jacket. He held a Schmeisser at the ready.

Von Berger moved past Hoffer. 'I'm *Sturmbannführer* von Berger. Who are you?'

'My name is Ritter – Hans Ritter – and thank God you're here. This is the fourth time I've done this run and it wasn't fun. Could I ask where we're going?'

'To the west, to Holstein Heath in *Schwarze Platz*. There's a castle, Schloss Adler, above Neustadt. Can we make it?'

'Yes. It's a three-hundred-mile flight and we'll have to refuel somewhere, but I'll tell you what, *Sturmbannführer*, I'd rather be there than here, so let's get the hell out of this place. Get your lads to open the doors.'

'A sound idea.'

Hoffer and Schneider opened the sliding door and Ritter climbed into the Storch and started the engine. The three men clambered in and Hoffer closed the door.

Outside, the fleeing refugees turned in astonishment, then fled to either side as the Storch bumped over rubble and glass and turned towards the Victory Column. The rain was torrential.

Ritter boosted power and roared down the avenue towards the Victory Column. People scattered, the Storch lifted, and at that moment, Russian artillery opened up, shells exploding on each side. The plane banked to starboard, narrowly missing the Victory Column, and rose up through the fog.

At two thousand feet, Ritter levelled off. 'We'll stay low until we're well away.'

When one looked down, there was only fire and artillery bursts and drifting smoke and fog. Hoffer said, 'It looks like hell on earth. I can't believe we're out of it.'

Von Berger got two cigarettes from his silver case, lit them and passed one back to Hoffer.

'So, you were right after all, Karl. It's Stalingrad all over again.'

Speaking above the roar of the engine, Ritter cried, 'As I said, it's three hundred miles to Holstein Heath, and I'm very low on fuel. I'm going to make for the Luftwaffe base at Rechlin.'

'That's fine by me,' von Berger told him. 'If you think it wise.'

'It is. We have no idea what's going to be available to us along the way. Mind you, it all depends on the weather at Rechlin. We'll see.'

* * *

21

Some time later, he descended through the torrential rain and fog and called in. 'Rechlin Tower. This is Captain Ritter, out of Berlin. Must land to refuel.'

There was a crackle of static and a voice said, 'I suggest you try elsewhere, Captain. The fog's bad here. We're down to four hundred metres.'

'I'm dangerously short of fuel.'

'The visibility's getting worse all the time, believe me.'

Ritter turned to von Berger inquiringly. The Baron selected another cigarette and Hoffer lit it for him. Von Berger blew out smoke and said to Ritter, 'We got out of Stalingrad and we've got out of Berlin. Everything else is a bonus. Let's do it.'

'At your orders, *Sturmbannführer*.'

The Storch descended very quickly, nothing but the fog surrounding them, and the driving rain, a grey, impenetrable world. Von Berger had no fear, too much had happened already – some strange destiny was surely at work. Even at four hundred metres, there was nothing.

He cried out to Ritter above the noise of the engine, 'Go for it. What've we got to lose?'

Ritter nodded, a strange fixed smile on his face, took the Storch down, and suddenly at a suicidal level of three hundred metres the Luftwaffe base of Rechlin came into view: the buildings, the hangars, two runways. There was evidence of bombing and two aircraft burned at the side of the runway, an old Dornier and a Ju 885 night fighter. A fire crew was in the middle of dousing the flames.

Ritter made a perfect landing and taxied past the astonished fire crew to the hangars and switched off.

'Well, that was close.'

'You're a genius, Ritter.'

'No, sir. It's just that now and then one gets better, usually when it's needed.'

As they got out, a field car drove up, a Luftwaffe colonel at the wheel. He got out. 'Good God, it's you, Ritter. Straight from Berlin? I can't believe you got out. How are things?'

'You wouldn't want to know. This is *Sturmbannführer* Baron Max von Berger and his boys.' He turned to von Berger. 'Colonel Strasser is an old friend.'

'May I enquire about your purpose, Baron?' Strasser asked.

Von Berger opened the briefcase and took out the Führer Directive, which he passed across. Strasser read it and noted the signature.

'Your credentials are impeccable, Baron. How may I assist?'

'We need refuelling for an onward flight to Holstein Heath.'

'I can handle that, all right. We've still got plenty of fuel and you are welcome to our hospitality, but there's no way you're going anywhere for some time. Just look.' He waved towards the runway, the fog rolling in at ground level.

'I'll see that you're refuelled and checked out, but there's no guarantee of departure. You can use the officers' mess, and in the unusual circumstances, your men may join you. I'll drive you all there.'

'I'll stay with the plane for the moment,' Ritter said. 'Make sure everything is okay.'

Strasser got behind the wheel of the field car. Von Berger and his two men got in and they drove away.

The mess was strangely desolate, an orderly at the bar, another acting as a waiter. He brought Hoffer and Schneider stew and bread and beer, and they sat by the window and ate.

Schneider said, 'I can't believe I'm out of Berlin. It's like a mad dream.'

'Where are you from?' Hoffer asked.

'Hamburg.'

'Which isn't looking too good these days. You're better off with us.'

23

Behind them, in a corner by the bar, the waiter served von Berger with ham sandwiches and crusty bread and salad. Strasser came back from his office to join him.

'Champagne,' he told the waiter and turned to von Berger with a smile. 'We're lucky. We've still got good booze and decent food. I don't think that will last.'

'Well, at least it's the Yanks and the Brits who are coming, not the Russians.'

'You can say that again.' They sampled the champagne when it came and started on the sandwiches, and Ritter joined them.

'Everything's being taken care of, but I can't see us getting off for a few hours. What's going to happen to you, Strasser?'

The colonel poured him a glass of champagne.

'Gentlemen, I don't know what your mission for the Führer is and I don't want to know. Personally, I await the arrival of the Americans with every fibre of my being.' He toasted them. 'To you, my friends. It's been a hard war.'

There were plenty of staff rooms at headquarters, and they all helped themselves to beds. Von Berger, dozing, was awakened by Strasser at two-thirty in the morning.

'Time to go.'

Von Berger sat up. 'How is the weather?'

'The fog has cleared to a certain extent, but the rain is still bad. The word is that the Russians have totally encircled Berlin. That could pose a serious threat here. Let's hope the Yanks make it first.'

'Off we go, then.'

The Storch waited beside Runway One, Ritter with it, Hoffer and Schneider inside. Strasser got out of the field car and handed von Berger a bag. 'Sandwiches, sausages, a couple of bottles of booze. Good luck, my friend.' He shook von Berger's hand vigorously and suddenly embraced him. 'What in the hell were we all playing at? How did we get in such a mess?'

Von Berger was incredibly moved. 'Keep the faith. Things will change. Our time will come. I'll seek you out.'

Strasser was astonished. 'You mean that, Baron?'

'Of course. I'll find you, believe me. I shall repay your help this night.'

He clambered into the plane after Ritter, closed everything, and outside, Strasser put his heels together and gave him a military salute. Von Berger returned it. The plane roared down the runway and lifted into the murk.

Ritter had given von Berger earphones and a throat mike. He spoke to him now. 'I'll take it very carefully. With our low speed and the weather, it could be three and a half hours, maybe even four, to Holstein Heath. Most of the time, I'll fly at two or three thousand, maybe higher if the weather continues bad.'

'That's fine.'

The flight was difficult with the rain and the patchy fog, sometimes clear and at others swirling relentlessly. One hour, two, the whole trip became monotonous. Von Berger had passed the food bag to Hoffer, who opened it and handed the sandwiches and sausages around. The wine was cheap stuff with a screw cap and he poured it into paper cups. Even Ritter had some and held out his cup for a second helping.

'Come on, it won't do me any harm. I need whatever help I can get in this weather.'

Von Berger finished his food, knocked back his wine and lit a cigarette. Rain beat on the windows. It was the strangest of sensations hammering through the bad early morning weather. *What am I doing here?* he thought. *Is it a dream? I should be in Berlin.* He shook his head. *I should still be in Berlin.*

And then he thought: *But I'm not. I'm on the way home to see Elsa and little Otto and Karl will see his Lotte and the two girls. It's a miracle and it's because of the Führer. There must be a meaning to it.*

Ritter said, 'It's still a bit thick down here. I think we'll be okay. I'm going up to four thousand.'

'Fine.'

They came out through intermittent fog. It was clear up there and clear to the horizon, a full moon touching the edge of the early-morning clouds.

Suddenly, there was a roaring, and the Storch was thrown to one side in the turbulence as a plane banked away to starboard and returned to take up station on the starboard side. They could see the pilot in the cockpit, the Red Star on the fuselage.

'What have we got?' Ritter asked. 'Looks like a Yak fighter, the new model with cannon. That could damage us.'

'So what do we do?'

'Well, I'm really too slow for him, but that could also be an advantage. Planes that are too fast sometimes overshoot. I'll go down and hope he'll do something stupid.'

He banked, went down quickly to three thousand metres, then banked again to port, went to two. The Yak started to fire its cannon, but too soon, because of his excessive speed, and he overshot and banked away.

He came in again, and this time punched a couple of holes in the starboard wing and splintered the window. Ritter cried out and reared back and there was blood on his face.

Ritter said, 'I'm okay, it's just a splinter. It'll give me an interesting scar. I'm getting tired of this – I'm going down further. I'll show this bastard how to fly.'

He went hard, all the way, and levelled at five hundred feet. The Yak came in again on his tail and Ritter dropped his flaps. The Storch seemed to stand still, and the Yak had

26

to bank steeply to avoid hitting them and went down into the farmland. There was a mushroom of flame below and they flew on.

'I said you were a genius,' von Berger told him.

'Only some of the time.'

Von Berger turned to Hoffer. 'Get the battle pack open. Find a dressing for his face. Give him a morphine ampoule, too.'

Ritter said, 'Better not. I'll tell you what, however – open that other bottle, whatever it is.'

'I thought it was wine, but it's vodka,' Hoffer told him.

'Good. I'm always better flying on booze.'

It was perhaps five or five-thirty in the morning when they came in towards Holstein Heath, approaching at two thousand feet, the dark, mysterious forest below, the *Schwarze Platz*, villages dotted here and there, and then Neustadt and Schloss Adler above it on the hill.

Von Berger felt incredibly emotional as the plane banked, very low, Ritter searching for a suitable landing.

'There,' von Berger growled. 'The meadow by the castle.'

'I see it.' Ritter turned in, slowed and made a perfect landing, rolling to a halt.

In the quiet, it was Schneider who said, 'I still can't believe it. We were in Berlin and now we're here.'

Behind them, a few people were coming up hesitantly from the village as von Berger and the others got out of the plane. Von Berger stood holding Hitler's briefcase, as a dozen men and a few women approached.

The leader, an ageing white-headed man, almost recoiled, 'My God, it's you, Baron.'

'A surprise, Hartmann,' von Berger said. 'How are you?'

'Baron, what can I say?' Hartmann removed his cap, took von Berger's hand and kissed it. 'Such terrible times.' He turned to Hoffer. 'And you, Karl.'

Von Berger said, 'Here we are, safe by a miracle, from Berlin. I'll explain later, but first I must see the Baroness, and Karl, his Lotte and the girls.'

Hartmann actually broke into weeping. 'God help me, Baron, the news is bad. They are in the chapel at the Schloss.'

Von Berger froze. 'What do you mean?'

'Your wife and son, Baron. Lotte and her daughters and fifteen villagers are in the church awaiting burial.' He turned to Hoffer. 'I am so sorry.'

Hoffer was stunned, horror on his face. Von Berger said, 'Who did this thing?'

'SS.'

'I can't believe it.'

'*Einsatzgruppen.*'

Einsatzgruppen were not Waffen SS, but extermination squads recruited from the jails of Germany, many of the men Ukrainians. Von Berger had heard stories that in the last few weeks they had thrown off all restraints, started looting and killing on their own, but he had hardly believed it to be true.

He was moving in slow motion now. The dream was so bad it was unbelievable. He said to Hoffer, 'You go and see to your family and I'll see to mine.' He turned to Ritter. 'You'd better be off. My deepest thanks.'

'No,' Ritter said, 'I'll stand by you. I'll come with you, if I may.'

'That's kind, my friend.'

They went up the steep path to the Schloss, von Berger and Ritter, followed by old Hartmann, and came to the ancient chapel. Von Berger pushed the door, it creaked open and he smelled the church smell, saw the memorials to his ancestors and the main family mausoleum, its doors standing wide. A coffin stood there, the lid half back, his wife inside, with his young son cradled in her left arm. He gazed down at her calm face, noticed the bruises.

'What happened to her?'

'Baron, what can I say?' Hartmann asked.

'Tell me,' von Berger said. 'Was she violated?'

'Every woman in the village was, Baron. Then the Ukrainians got drunk and started shooting and the deaths happened.'

'How many of these bastards were there?'

'Twenty – twenty-one. They moved on to Plosen.'

Ten miles up the road through the forest.

'So, we know where they are.' Von Berger turned to Ritter. 'You can still go. I appreciate more than you know what you've done. As I told Strasser, things will change for all of us, and I'll search you out.'

Ritter's face, with the dressing on the cheek, was haggard. 'I've no intention of going.'

'Then go down to the village with Hartmann and make sure his truck is ready to leave. I have private business here.'

Ritter and Hartmann left. Von Berger stood by the mausoleum for a while, then went to the rear, where there were two statues of saints. His hand passed inside one, it groaned and creaked open. He slipped the Führer's briefcase inside, then closed the secret door. He leaned over, kissed his wife and son, and left.

In the village, the tenants waited and he passed amongst them, holding his hand out to be kissed, though not in arrogance; it was a tradition that had reigned in Holstein Heath for hundreds of years. These were his people, and the women who cried in despair did it because they looked to him for guidance.

Hoffer came to him, his face bleak. 'Your orders, Baron?'

'We're going to get these swine. Are you ready to leave, Hoffer?'

Before he could reply, young Schneider said, 'And me too, Baron.'

'Excellent.'

'And you can include me,' Ritter said. 'I can shoot a Schmeisser with the best of them.'

As chance would have it, it was at that moment that the Americans arrived.

Not that they were much of a force. It was a single jeep and the young captain in the passenger seat wore a steel helmet and combat gear. His shoulder patch indicated an Airborne Ranger. A sergeant was at the wheel. They rolled to a halt and sat there, watchful.

'Does anyone here speak English?' the captain asked.

'Of course,' the Baron said.

'Good. I'll take your surrender. My unit is about ten miles back. I'm Captain James Kelly, on forward reconnaissance. This is Sergeant Hanson.'

'And what might you be doing here?'

'Hey, buddy.' The driver picked up a submachine gun. 'Watch your mouth.'

Ritter and Hoffer and young Schneider raised their Schmeissers threateningly, and Kelly said to Hanson, 'Can it.' He spoke to von Berger. 'We have information that the castle would make a possible headquarters. Who are you, anyway?'

'*Sturmbannführer* Baron Max von Berger, owner of Schloss Adler and Holstein Heath.'

Kelly shook his head. 'Wait a minute. I've got a report that says von Berger's in the Bunker with Hitler. One of his aides or something.'

'True as of yesterday,' von Berger said. 'If you will look behind you at the meadows, you will notice the Storch in which Captain Hans Ritter here flew me and my two men out of Berlin.'

Kelly nodded. 'Okay, we'll argue about it later. You can all surrender your weapons now.'

'This is a great coup for you, Captain, but, if you don't mind, not just yet. We've urgent business to take care of first.'

'And what would that be?'

Max von Berger told him.

Kelly shook his head. 'That's a terrible thing, but you four guys are going to take on twenty-one of these bastards? You could get killed and I can't allow that to happen.'

'I see. I'm too valuable to lose?' Von Berger shook his head. 'It's been a long war, Captain. From El Alamein to Stalingrad, I've seen hell on earth, and for me the war is over. I don't want to kill you, but I must kill these men. I could not live with myself otherwise. So we will leave in the old woodcutter's truck, drive ten miles down to Plosen, and there we'll find the Ukrainians and get the business done.' He turned to Hoffer. 'You drive.'

Kelly started to say something, and then he stopped. 'Ah, hell, Baron, I guess I'd do the same thing. But afterwards . . .'

'You're an optimist, I see. All right, let's go.'

The road wound through dark, sombre forest all the way to Plosen. When they were close, they came across a crowd of women and older men moving along either side of the road. Hoffer pulled up and recognized the village mayor.

'Hey, Frankel, what's happening?'

'My God, it's you, Karl. These Ukrainians, we know what they did in Neustadt. Young Meyer escaped on his motorcycle, came and gave us warning. We all left in a hurry, faded into the forest. I hear they did terrible things.'

Von Berger got out and held out his hand. 'Frankel.'

The old man's eyes widened. 'Baron, this is unbelievable.' He kissed the hand. 'Meyer told me about the Baroness and your son.' He turned to Hoffer. 'And your Lotte?'

Kelly and Hanson came round from the jeep, and Ritter and Schneider joined them. Kelly said, 'What's happening?'

31

'The Mayor of Plosen is just about to tell us,' von Berger said in English, then in German, 'Where are they, Frankel?'

'I stayed close to observe. They came in two trucks and a *Kubelwagen*. They rampaged round the village and discovered two young women. Then they went to the inn, the White Stag. I could hear shouting, breaking glass. They're all drunk.'

'Any guards?' Hoffer asked.

'Not that I could see.'

Von Berger patted his shoulder. 'Take care of your people and I'll take care of these animals.'

'But, Baron, there are twenty-four of them.'

'Really? I thought it was twenty-one.' He turned to Ritter, Schneider and Hoffer. 'So, that's six for each of us. Can we manage that?'

'Haven't we always, Baron?' Hoffer opened a battle pack, took out double ammunition clips taped together and handed them to Ritter and Schneider.

Von Berger opened his black leather coat, took the Luger from his holster, checked it and put it in his right-hand pocket. 'Have you a spare, Karl?'

Hoffer produced a Mauser from the battle pack and handed it over. Von Berger put it in the left-hand pocket of his coat.

'Twenty-four of these bastards and four of you. That's odds of six to one,' Kelly said.

Von Berger smiled, grimly. 'We're Waffen SS. We're used to it.' He clapped Schneider on the shoulder. 'He's only a boy, but he knows how to do the job. Six to one? So what? Take your camouflage blouse off, Karl.' Hoffer did so, and Kelly saw the medals, the paratrooper's badge, a single Knight's Cross at the throat.

'You will also have observed that Captain Ritter has the Knight's Cross. It's been a long war and it's had a bad ending, but you must understand one thing. We intend to kill these

32

Ukrainians, all twenty-four. Kill them.' He turned to his men. 'Is this not so?'

Even Ritter got his heels together as they gave the answer: *Jawohl, Sturmbannführer.*

He ignored Kelly completely now. 'Let's go,' and they scrambled into the truck and drove away.

As the jeep followed, Hanson said, 'That guy is crazy, they all are.'

Kelly nodded. 'Absolutely.' He took the Colt from his holster and started to reload it as they followed the truck.

They paused in the trees and looked down at the White Stag. It was quite large and very ancient, with the village church and a graveyard behind. Kelly glanced through field glasses at the two trucks and the *Kubelwagen*. There was no sign of guards, but the noise of drunken laughter drifted up. He passed the field glasses to von Berger, who had a look. He handed them back.

'I'll go in the front door, which will put them off balance. They are, after all, supposed to be under SS authority. I suggest the rest of you go by the graveyard.' He said to Ritter, 'Karl knows it well. The bar is very large. There are two rear entrances via the kitchen and side windows.' He turned to Kelly. 'One favour. I'll borrow your Jeep to drive up to the door. You two can stay here and my friends will approach on foot.'

Kelly shook his head. 'No, I won't lend you the Jeep. But I will drive it.' He turned to Hanson. 'Give me that Thompson. I'll see you later – maybe.'

'Go to hell,' Hanson said. 'With all due respect, sir. I've been fighting since D-Day. A walk through a graveyard with the SS sounds just about right.'

Kelly and von Berger waited to give them a chance to slip down through the edge of the forest and move behind the church into the graveyard. Von Berger watched for movement through the glasses.

'Now,' he said, and Kelly drove them down the hill and parked beside the other vehicles.

Von Berger led the way up the steps, pulling on his leather gloves, and Kelly followed, holding the Thompson across his chest. Von Berger eased open the door and stepped in, followed by Kelly.

The Ukrainians were scattered around the room, some sitting at tables, a number standing at the bar, a couple behind the bar serving drinks. The leader was a *Hauptsturmführer*, a brute of a man in a soiled uniform, his face dirty and unshaven. He had a young woman on each knee, their clothes torn, faces bruised, eyes swollen from weeping. One by one, the men noticed von Berger and stopped talking.

There was total silence. Von Berger stood there, his legs apart, his hands in the pockets of the black leather coat, holding it apart, displaying that magnificent uniform, the medals.

'Your name?'

'Gorsky,' the *Hauptsturmführer* said, as a kind of reflex.

'Ah. Ukrainian.'

It was the way von Berger said it that the Ukrainian didn't like. 'And who the hell are you?'

'Your superior officer, *Sturmbannführer* Baron Max von Berger. It was my wife, Baroness von Berger, and my son, along with fifteen others, that you butchered at Schloss Adler and Neustadt.'

Men were already reaching for weapons. Kelly lifted his Thompson, and suddenly Gorsky pulled the two girls across his knees in front of him so that only half his face showed.

'So what are you going to do about it? Take them, boys,' he shouted.

Von Berger's hand came out of his right pocket with the Luger and he shot Gorsky twice in the left side of the skull, narrowly missing the girls who dropped to the floor as Gorsky went backwards in the chair.

The carnage began, Kelly spraying the bar area. A side window crashed open and Ritter and Hanson fired through. Some of the Ukrainians turned to run and flung open the doors to the kitchen, only to find Hoffer and Schneider. There was an exchange of fire, but not for long. There were dead men everywhere, just a few still moving. Hanson had stopped a bullet in the shoulder and Schneider in his left arm.

Von Berger took the Mauser from his other pocket and tossed it to Hoffer. 'Karl. Finish them.'

'For God's sake,' Kelly said.

'It is his right.'

Hoffer found five men still alive and shot each one in the head. The girls had run for it, screaming. Ritter had opened a battle pack and was putting a field dressing on Hanson, while Schneider waited.

Kelly surveyed the bodies. 'So that's it?'

'No. Now we go home and bury our dead. After that, we are yours to dispose of.' Von Berger put a hand on Kelly's shoulder. 'I am in your debt eternally. I *will* repay you.'

'Repay me?' Kelly was mystified.

'A matter of honour.'

He was, of course, handled personally by top officers in both British and American Intelligence, since he had been one of Hitler's aides in those last few months in the Bunker. His account of events was fascinating and recorded in the smallest detail, but for Allied intelligence there was a problem with Max von Berger. On the one hand, he was unquestionably SS, and a commander. On the other, he was a brave and gallant soldier who seemed never to have involved himself in the more unsavoury aspects of the Nazi regime. Never involved himself in anything remotely connected with the

Jewish pogroms. In fact, it was soon established that he had had a dangerous secret all along – one of von Berger's great grandmothers on the maternal side had been Jewish.

He had also never been a member of the Nazi Party, though it was true that most of the German population had also not been members of the party.

Which left only the question of the flight out of Berlin. Obviously, von Berger mentioned nothing to them of his interview with the Führer. Indeed, he had put together a reasonable story with Ritter, while they were still together.

The story was this: Ritter had been ordered to Berlin in the Storch as a back-up plane in case there were problems with the Arado assigned to fly out the new Luftwaffe commander, von Greim. There had been no problems, however. Von Berger, as one of Hitler's aides, knowing that the plane was languishing in Goebbels' garage and that the end was only hours away, had seized the opportunity to get out and had taken two of his men with him.

It was a perfectly simple explanation. There was no reason not to accept it, and Ritter backed it to the hilt, and so, in the end, that was that. As prisoners of war, they were disposed of in various ways. Many were sent to England for farm work. Amongst them was Max von Berger, who was posted to a camp in Hampshire. The regulations were minimal and each day he was allocated to a local manor house and its home farm, along with several other prisoners. There was nothing unusual in this. Officers up to the level of general found themselves working in such a way.

The truth was that the other prisoners deferred to him, called him 'Herr Baron' with respect, and the owner of the estate, an ageing Lord, soon realized he had someone special on board, and not only that, a countryman by nature.

Before long, he was running things. The war was over, the villagers in Hawkley were decent people, and gradually the

Germans were accepted, even for a pint in the pub. And then, at the end of 1947, German prisoners began to be returned home and amongst them was Max von Berger.

It was snowing when he arrived in Neustadt off the local bus. As it drove away he went up the steps, a bag in his hand, and entered the inn, the Eagle. Local men were in there drinking beer, some eating, and he saw old Hartmann by the bar and Karl Hoffer and young Schneider at a table nearby eating stew. Someone turned and saw him.

'My God, Baron.'

Everyone turned, the entire room went still. Hoffer moved first, jumping up, running to meet him, in an excess of emotion, embracing him.

'Baron, we wondered where you were. I've been back six months and brought Schneider with me. His entire family were killed in the bombing in Hamburg.'

Von Berger put an arm around Schneider, who was actually sobbing. 'Come on, boy, we got out of Berlin, didn't we? There's nothing to cry about.'

He called to the landlord, 'The bill's on me, my friend, let the beer flow.'

He turned to Hoffer. 'I'm so pleased to see you. Let's sit down.'

In a corner booth, they talked, young Schneider listening. 'We're getting by,' Hoffer said. 'It's mainly subsistence farming, but we're all in it together. Everyone is taken care of.'

'And you?'

'Well, I act as bailiff. It gives me something to do.'

'You haven't . . .'

'Found someone? No, Baron.'

'What about the Schloss?'

'We had the Americans for two years, so it's in good condition. The thing you don't know about is the . . . situation with Holstein Heath.'

'And what would that be?'

'When the border between the East and West was agreed on by the Allies, we should have been inside the Eastern zone, and Communist.'

'I thought we were in the Western zone?'

'Well, no, that's it. We aren't there either. The whole of the estate isn't in either of the zones. Someone made a mistake drafting the map.'

Max von Berger was astonished. 'You mean we're a kind of independent state?' He laughed out loud. 'Like Monaco?'

Hoffer, an intelligent man, said, 'Well, not exactly. The police are technically West German. However, they're all local boys, mostly ex-army or SS, so they see things our way.'

'Excellent.' Von Berger drained his beer and stood up. 'Show me the Schloss.'

Hoffer did, and he'd been right. It was run down, but the Americans hadn't kicked it to pieces. Finally, they approached the chapel. It was dark in the early winter evening, but candles flickered close to the mausoleum. Von Berger stood and looked and noticed some winter roses.

'Who are those from?'

'Village women. They like to keep things right. It's the same at the church for the others, my wife, the girls.'

Von Berger said, 'That day, Karl, those final killings. It wasn't that I was leaving it to you. I felt you had a greater right.'

'I know that, Baron.'

'Do you ever regret what we did?'

'Never.'

'Good. Now, pay attention. We were comrades then and comrades now, and I am going to share my greatest secret with you.'

He went behind the mausoleum and pressed the hidden catch. The statue groaned and moved. Von Berger reached in and took out the briefcase.

'This is the true reason we left Berlin.' He opened it and extracted the blue book. 'This is Hitler's diary, Karl.'

'My God in Heaven,' Hoffer gasped. 'Can this be true?'

'Yes. I'll tell you later what's in it, but right now we'll put it back.'

He pressed the catch and the statue reversed into place. He fastened the briefcase and held it up.

'And in here is the solution to all our financial problems. I'll explain it to you as we go. The first thing we must do is visit Berger Steel. We'll need decent suits and some sort of vehicle.'

'I've still got a *Kubelwagen* from the war, Baron.'

'Excellent. Stuttgart then, but Geneva first. That's where the money is.'

Geneva was amazingly easy. At the bank, the passwords and codes from the material given to him by the Führer inspired immediate compliance. The rather ordinary-looking banker indicated how immense the resources were at his disposal, and he transferred ten million into a liquid personal account, thus establishing his name and status. The bank, in effect, jumped to attention.

His next move was to contact Berger Steel's lawyers in Munich, leading to a meeting on-site at the Stuttgart factory. They toured it with the general manager, Heinz. It was working, of course, but in a low-key manner, a certain amount of steel-making, but not much more than that.

'As you can still see, we had bomb damage, but on the whole we were lucky and we've an excellent workforce,' Heinz told him.

The lawyer, Henry Abel, said, 'Cash flow and investment, that's the trouble. We don't have enough of either.'

'Not any more.' Von Berger turned to Heinz. 'I'm transferring five million into the company accounts tomorrow.'

'Dear God, Baron,' Heinz said, 'I'll guarantee you results with that kind of money.'

And so it proved. Over the years, the company contributed more than most to the miracle that became West Germany. As they developed into one of the most important steelworks, von Berger diversified into construction, hotels, the developing post-war leisure industry.

Soon his tentacles moved westward to the United States, his hotel interests burgeoning, and an ex-Airborne Ranger officer turned New York attorney named James Kelly proved more than useful, eventually becoming head of legal affairs for the American branch of Berger International.

At an early stage, he sought out Colonel Strasser, as he had promised, and Strasser became an adept troubleshooter, eventually overseeing all personnel matters for Berger. Ritter had been a different case. As usual with many wartime pilots, Ritter had been unable to do without the adrenaline rush, so though Berger had kept him as a personal pilot, it was never enough, and one day in 1960, Ritter, performing at an airshow in an Me 109, stalled for the last time and plunged into the ground. At the funeral, they stood together, the Baron, Schneider, Hoffer, Strasser and Kelly, who had flown over from the States.

'Thirty-eight years old, and after all that he did,' Strasser said, 'I'd say that's young. It frankly makes me uneasy.'

Schneider, always 'Young Schneider' to them, said, 'That Berlin flight was amazing. We shouldn't even be here now.'

'Well, we are, and the work continues,' the Baron said.

As the Cold War extended, the position of the great estate of Holstein Heath became more ambivalent, but von Berger's position as one of West Germany's leading industrialists gave him the right international contacts needed to block anything the East German regime could do.

The estate had developed a prosperity beyond belief, with Karl Hoffer as general manager, and young Schneider as his assistant. Von Berger poured in money, and totally refurbished the castle, using the apparently inexhaustible funds from Geneva. He even had a runway constructed in the meadow, big enough for small planes to land.

Any overt support of Nazi ideals was not part of his agenda. It would have been counterproductive anyway, but gradually over the years there was a quiet coming together of others whose names were on the lists in Hitler's briefcase. Not the *Kameradenwerk*, the Action for Comrades that Hitler had mentioned, but a sort of secret brotherhood, almost like a Masonic order, with Max von Berger as a kind of godfather. Anyone with the right background, the right ideas, could turn to him and get a hearing, a handout, help. Always discreet, always reasonable, a legend to the former soldiers of the German Army, there was nothing the authorities could complain of.

The truth was that the brutal death of his wife and son had killed something inside him in a single devastating moment. He had taken his revenge, which had proved no revenge. It had, as he'd read in a poem, made of his heart a stone, left him curiously lacking in emotion.

The years rolled on, and in 1970 that emotionally cold heart found release when, at forty-eight years of age, he formed an attachment for a young Italian woman named Maria Rossi. Attractive and clever, with a degree in accounting, she became a personal assistant, travelling the world with him, and the inevitable happened.

Von Berger fought against his feelings for her, for it seemed a betrayal of his wife, but before he had to make any final decision, the situation resolved itself. She left him quite suddenly, leaving behind a brief apologetic letter telling him that family business had called her away to Palermo. He never heard from her again.

Time went by, and people started to die on him. First, Schneider was killed in a stupid accident on the estate when a tractor he was driving turned over, crushing him to death. Strasser went next with lung cancer, ten years later.

Von Berger went to the funeral with Hoffer. It was 1982 and he was sixty.

'The grim reaper is spacing things out, Karl, have you noticed?'

'It had occurred to me, Baron.'

Hoffer had remarried in middle life: a cousin, a widow from the village. She had died of a heart attack only a year before. He was two years older than von Berger. 'So what do we do?'

'Gird our loins. I've been thinking of going into the arms business, and there's always oil, especially with Russia opening up.'

'May I ask why you need to do that, Baron,' Hoffer said patiently. 'You already have enormous wealth.'

'My dear Karl, more than even you could imagine. But my life lacks purpose, Karl. There is an emptiness I cannot fill. Maria Rossi made me warm for a while, and then went. This void in me – I must fill it, and work and enterprise are the only way.' He clapped Hoffer on the shoulder. 'Don't worry about me, Karl. I'll sort it out.'

The following day, back at the Schloss, he visited the chapel, opened the secret place, and leafed through the Hitler diary. He had read it so many times that he almost knew it by heart. There had never been any occasion to use it and as he replaced it now, he wondered if there ever would be.

He sat there for a while by the mausoleum, thinking of his wife and son, then took a deep breath and stood up. So, Russian oilfields and armaments. So be it. And he went out.

By 1992, he was seventy, his holdings in Russian oil extensive because of the temporary loss of the Kuwaiti oilfields in the Gulf War and the embargoes placed on Iraqi oil. The money simply poured in, and the continuing threat in the Middle East and India and Pakistan made for more and more lucrative deals in the arms business.

In both Britain and the United States, there was unease at the highest level about his various dealings, but he didn't care. He was now head of a consortium so staggeringly wealthy that his power was immense.

In 1997, James Kelly died in New York, but later in the same year, the Baron suffered his greatest blow of all when Karl Hoffer passed away with a heart attack.

The open coffin was on display in the chapel. Sitting beside it, alone, his hands on the silver handle of the cane he needed to get around these days, he thought of their years together in the war and that last final flight from Berlin.

'So, it would appear I am the last, old friend. My hip bothers me a great deal these days. You remember our old wartime motto: to the men of the SS, nothing is impossible.' He sighed, then gathered himself together. 'So back to work.'

He limped out, and the chapel door slammed behind him. It was quiet, lit only by the guttering candles. Little did he know that just around the corner, a series of events were waiting that would change his life as surely as their flight from Berlin.

LONDON
THE EMPTY QUARTER
IRAQ

3

The following year was the first time he met Paul Rashid, the Earl of Loch Dhu. The legendary figure behind Rashid Investments, the Earl had had an English mother and an Omani general for a father, and had served in the SAS during the Gulf War. The Rashid wealth was well known, as was their grip on the oilfields of Hazar, and also in the Dhofar, for Paul Rashid was Bedu and controlled the vast deserts of the Empty Quarter.

Berger International had sought oil concessions in the Dhofar, but even the Americans hadn't been able to break the iron control of the Rashids. The Baron tried a different approach. He arranged an arms deal with Yemen, then asked Rashid Investments to broker it for him, reporting directly to him. In this way, he hoped, of course, to get to meet Paul Rashid, and one day he received a message that the chairman would meet him in the Piano Bar at the Dorchester Hotel.

He arrived in the early evening as stipulated, and ordered a whiskey – an Irish. He'd always favoured that. He sat, hands on the handle of his cane, and noticed a supremely beautiful woman pause at the entrance. She wore a black jumpsuit, her black hair hanging to her shoulders and framing a face that could have belonged to the Queen of Sheba. And then she came down the steps and approached him.

'Baron von Berger?'

'Why, yes.' He started to rise.

'No, don't get up.' She pulled a chair forward. 'I'm Lady Kate Rashid.'

He was totally thrown. 'My dear young lady, I was expecting Lord Loch Dhu.'

'But you asked for a meeting with the chairman of Rashid Investments, and that's me. My brother prefers to stay in the shadows, so to speak.' She laughed. 'Don't look so surprised. I did manage to get an MA at Oxford. Now let's have a glass of champagne and you can tell me how we can possibly help the great Baron Max von Berger to do something he can't do for himself.'

She called to Giuliano, the bar manager, and ordered house champagne. 'Don't worry, it's the best in the place, but then everything here is the best. So, Baron . . .'

'Well, as you may know, Berger International dabbles in the arms business.'

'I wouldn't call it dabbling, Baron.'

'It's not quite on a par with your oil interests.' He smiled. 'I have an order from the Yemeni government for assorted weaponry. Ten million pounds' worth. It's no big deal, but the shipment is Russian in origin, so I was hoping to bring it down from the Black Sea in a Greek-owned freighter to Aden.'

'Let me guess. Suddenly there are difficulties with the port authorities in Aden, greedy hands held out.'

'You are a very perceptive young lady.'

'A realist, Baron.'

'Who understands the Arab mentality.'

'I do not regard myself as Arab, Baron, and not just because I am half-English.'

'I am well aware of that. Your family is as great in England as my own is in Germany. I meant no slight.'

'Of course you didn't, but, as I said, that's not what I meant. My other half is Bedu, and that is different from being Arab. We bow our heads to no one. The Bedu are the real power in Hazar and the Dhofar, but especially in the Empty Quarter. The Bedu control the Empty Quarter, and the Rashid control the Bedu. My brother is the undisputed leader.'

'A remarkable man, the Earl, and the rise in Rashid Investments has been equally remarkable. And yet he is not so often on the scene, as it were.'

'As I told you, he prefers to stay in the shadows. I have two brothers, George and Michael, who are managing directors. And, as you know, I am chairman.'

'And Paul?'

'He prefers to spend time in Hazar with the Bedu. To them, he is a great warrior. He roams the desert by camel, lives in the old Bedu way, guarded by men who would die for him, burned by the sun. He eats dates and dried meats. Would you eat dates and dried meats, Baron?'

Giuliano had materialized with a waiter and thumbed the cork off a bottle of Dorchester champagne.

Max von Berger laughed out loud. 'To be frank, I'd rather enjoy the delights of the Piano Bar.'

'Then taste the champagne for me.'

'Only if you allow me one privilege.'

'And what would that be?'

'To call you Kate. It's a delightful name and suits you beyond measure.'

She smiled. 'My pleasure, Max.'

He laughed again and nodded to Guiliano, who smiled and poured. 'So where are we, Kate?'

'Regarding your arms shipment? It's no problem, but we can do better than the Greek freighter. I'll provide a Rashid

49

ship with an Arab crew. I'll sort out the Aden end of things, and provide security for the cargo, including its deployment up-country.'

'And what will I have to pay for such munificence?'

'Twenty-five per cent.'

There was a moment's pause, then von Berger smiled. 'What a remarkable young woman you are, Kate. I accept, of course.'

'No contract, no handshake?'

'My word.' He raised his glass. 'To you, my dear, and to the future.'

They clinked glasses and drank. She nodded to Giuliano, who came forward to refill and then she sat back, watching the Baron calmly. She knew everything about him, or at least thought she did. He intrigued her, everything about him, and she enchanted him: not in some silly superficial way, a seventy-six-year-old man falling for a beautiful young woman. It was just that everything about her was so remarkable.

'To the future, you say?' She smiled. 'So now we come to it. Your interests in the Russian oilfields are not enough. You seek oil concessions in the Dhofar.'

It was a statement. He said, 'Alas, to no purpose. The Russians have tried, the Americans, even a British consortium.'

'So now, by coincidence, we have Max von Berger of Berger International coming to Rashid hoping to meet my brother to broker a piffling little ten million arms deal.'

Von Berger hadn't enjoyed himself so much in years. He laughed again. 'I surrender completely. I thought if I met your brother, it might make a difference.'

'Then why didn't you say so? You're interested in the Dhofar and development. So are we. You want to discuss this with Paul? I'll arrange it. We'll fly in a company Gulfstream to Hazar – say, ten tomorrow morning? We'll go up-country by helicopter to Shabwa Oasis in the Empty

50

Quarter, and my brother will see you there. Does any of this seem acceptable?'

'Only that if I was forty years younger, I'd have been at your feet.'

'Oh, very nice, especially coming from the pick of the SS. So it's a date. Now, as our business here is concluded, what about taking me somewhere nice for dinner? The Ivy would be acceptable. All those awful celebrities make it so interesting.'

And Max von Berger, filled with excitement, pushed himself up and clicked his heels.

'Lady Kate Rashid, the pleasure is all mine.'

The following day, the Rashid Gulfstream landed in Hazar at the military base, a relic of British imperialism. A Hawk helicopter was waiting and Kate led the way to it, von Berger following. He hadn't felt so alive in years. So much of the time on the flight from Northolt had been spent in conversation about every subject under the sun. He was totally fascinated by her.

The flight in the helicopter was noisy and uncomfortable, as it carved a way through the great heat, bouncing in the thermals over the vastness, the desolation of the Empty Quarter. Evening was falling, the huge sand dunes stretched to infinity, or so it seemed, and von Berger loved it, all of it. Age seemed to have slipped away from him.

And then, in the distance, in the gloom, there were fires, and finally, the Hawk swept in over the vast Shabwa Oasis and hovered. It was a great pool surrounded by palm trees, herds of camels and goats, and an enormous encampment; women, children and men, all Bedu, milling around.

The helicopter landed, the engine stopped. The pilot opened the door and stood to one side. 'Here we are then, Baron.' Kate smiled. 'If you would follow me.'

She was wearing a khaki bush shirt and trousers. Now she pulled on a headcloth and stepped out. The crowd had stepped back and Rashid warriors ran forward with rifles, making a line. The silence was almost total, except for the snort of a camel and the plaintive bleating of the goats. Then down the lane came Paul Rashid, a dramatic figure in head-cloth and black robes.

He held out his arms. 'Little sister.' Kate ran to him for his embrace.

The crowd erupted, the noise deafening, Paul Rashid turned to von Berger and held out his hand. 'You must excuse their enthusiasm, Baron. My sister has a special place in their hearts.'

'I find that perfectly understandable.'

Rashid's grip tightened, then he leaned forward and kissed von Berger on each cheek.

'Excuse the familiarity, but witnessed by my people, this makes you special, too. Inviolate, you might say. Word spreads easily in the Empty Quarter, better than on a computer. You will always be safe here.'

To von Berger, it was so familiar. It was like Holstein Heath, the dark place, the special relationship with his people. He was very moved.

'You make me proud, my Lord.'

Rashid turned to the crowd. 'This is Baron von Berger, my friend.'

The crowd raised their voices, the camels wheezed, every-thing was in motion. Kate turned to von Berger. 'Just go with the flow, and remember from now on you are the guest of every Bedu in the Empty Quarter.'

'So, a little hospitality would be in order,' Paul Rashid said. 'First, you must refresh yourself after the journey, then we eat.'

'And then comes business,' Kate said.

'Enough for now.' Paul Rashid turned and led the way through the crowd.

* * *

The Baron was taken to a richly furnished tent, with carpets and hangings. A canvas bath was provided, two young men on hand who spoke English and attended his every need.

Later he was taken to a larger tent, filled with people eating and sitting on cushions in the traditional way, women bringing in food of many kinds from the cooking tent: stews, roasted lambs, an absolute feast. Von Berger sat between Rashid and Kate.

Rashid said, 'I trust you understand. My people expect this. They have their traditions, Baron.'

'Max,' von Berger told him. 'Please call me Max.' He reached for a dish of some sort of lamb chops a woman offered, took one with his bare hand and tried it. 'Delicious.' He turned to Paul Rashid. 'One old soldier to another: I was in the Winter War in Russia and this is infinitely better.'

Paul Rashid smiled, 'Then enjoy, my friend.'

Much later, they sat, the three of them, by a blazing fire, guards sitting close by, drinking coffee, AK47s across their knees.

Rashid said, 'So, this Yemeni arms affair. Of course we'll broker it for you. No big deal. But let's be frank. What my sister said to you was true. This Yemeni thing is nothing to you, we know that. What you are interested in are oil concessions, in the Empty Quarter perhaps and certainly in the Dhofar.'

'Absolutely. I know that the Russians are after it, the Brits, the Americans, but your influence with the Bedu confounds them all.'

'That's true.'

There was silence. The Baron said, 'Would you happen to have a cigarette?'

'Of course. I'll have one with you.' He called in Arabic, a youth ran forward, and cigarettes were provided, and a lighter.

'They got me through the Winter War, these things,' the Baron said.

'And me the Gulf War,' Rashid replied. 'We have much in common.'

Von Berger turned to Kate. 'Listen to what I say. I would value your opinion.'

'Of course.'

'Right. If I try to obtain concessions in the Dhofar, the great powers would put in place as many roadblocks as they could. Even now, the Russian government isn't happy with my holdings in their country. Any extension of my power would displease them.'

'That would seem obvious,' she said.

'And the Americans have always distrusted me. The Hitler business never goes away.' He turned to Rashid. 'You, on the other hand, they are stuck with. That intrigues me. Why haven't you used those concessions in the Dhofar?'

Rashid drank his coffee. 'Tell him,' he said to Kate.

'Cash flow,' she said. 'Rashid Investments is worth billions, but it's all tied up. Capital investment, mainly. I don't need to tell you that oil exploration is an expensive business.'

'But if you had the resources, you could go ahead in the Dhofar. America and Russia could do nothing.'

She looked at him calmly. 'We'd need a lot of money. And I wouldn't want it tied up by the banks.'

'What she means is we'd need something like one billion in cash, nice and fluid in our own account, to get started,' Paul Rashid said.

Von Berger nodded. 'Two billion would be better.'

They both stared at him. 'Two billion?' Kate said.

'Yes. Let's see, today is Tuesday. I'll set the wheels in motion, you could have it by Friday.' He smiled. 'And then you would be developing oil in the Dhofar, not me. The White House, the Kremlin, Downing Street – they wouldn't know a thing.'

It was Kate who answered. 'Oh, God, that would be beautiful.'

Her brother held up his hand. 'This is not a joke. You're not that kind of man.'

'No, I'm not renowned for my sense of humour where money is concerned.'

'But the manipulations necessary to raise such a sum on the international finance scene would be very obvious. There is no way the Americans, the Russians and the Brits would not be aware of it.'

'No, there you're wrong. There would be no need for anything unusual to happen. I have access to unlimited cash funds.'

Kate was astonished. 'In that amount? But from where?'

'Oh, Swiss banks. I'm what is known as cash-rich. There'll be no wheeler-dealing on the stock exchanges, no haggling for loans or investments in the financial markets. Just healthy injections of cash into Rashid Investments, as you choose.'

They looked at each other. Kate was excited and clutched at her brother's arm. 'Paul, we'll never have such a chance again. We can confound them all.'

'I know, little sister.' Rashid turned to von Berger. 'And in return?'

'In return, I would expect to be made a silent partner in Rashid Investments.'

'On what terms?'

'Nothing onerous, nothing unreasonable. We can work it out together, here, and I'll step back. In fact, we shouldn't even meet socially, not ever again.' He turned to Kate. 'Which will be a great deprivation.'

Paul Rashid sat brooding. After a while, he said, 'Those international oil cartels, they'd love to drill anywhere they damn well pleased in the Dhofar and walk all over the Bedu in the process. Rape the desert.'

'And you would do it differently?'

'It can be done differently, Max, no one knows that better than you. You are right, by the way. We can't be seen together in the future.'

'So, we have a deal?'

'Subject to our agreement on the partnership, yes. I'll arrange all the necessary documentation and you will arrange the funding.'

'By Friday.'

'We have an ancient Bedu custom, more binding than any contract.' Rashid took a small razor-sharp knife from his belt. 'Your thumb, Baron, the left hand.' Von Berger held out the hand, Rashid touched the end of the thumb and drew a spot of blood. He did the same to his own, then touched it to von Berger's, their blood mingling.

Kate held out her left hand. 'Me, too. It is my right. I brought him.'

He smiled. 'And you did well, little sister.' He pricked her thumb also and she touched his and then von Berger's. Paul Rashid leaned forward and put an arm about both of them. 'This bond that will last for life itself.'

'I swear it on my honour,' von Berger said.

Kate smiled and something glowed in her eyes. 'What a pity, Max, that we can't meet again, but Paul is right.'

'No more Piano Bar.' He spread his hands. 'I'm desolate.'

Little did he know, but some two years later, he was to meet her again and under the most dramatic of circumstances.

January 2000, to be precise. Von Berger was approached through his Berlin offices by Iraqi government sources. They wanted exploratory talks regarding arms supplies. Von Berger wasn't surprised. Arms dealers all over the world had been approached. There wasn't much chance of keeping quiet about it with the Israeli Mossad so closely allied to American and British intelligence.

He wasn't certain why he went to Iraq at all. He didn't approve of Saddam Hussein or his regime. The lift that Kate Rashid had given to his life had been only temporary. Since the meeting in Hazar, he had not had any overt contact with the Rashids. The business dealings in the Dhofar, in which he had invested so much, had prospered hugely. The truth was that he was seventy-eight years old, and the only people he had cared about were dead and gone. He had accomplished so much and there was nothing left that was worth doing. He was also bored, so he went to Baghdad.

The city seemed immense, ancient and yet modern, hot and dusty, crowded with humanity. He flew into the airport in a Gulfstream, and was received with extreme courtesy by a young intelligence major called Aroun, immaculate in a khaki uniform that looked as if it had been tailored in London's Savile Row. Sporting medals and the wings of a paratrooper, he was handsome, intelligent and spoke good English. He eased von Berger through the usual formalities and escorted him out to a limousine, a Lincoln. He joined him in the rear seat.

'Do you smoke, Baron?' He offered his cigarette case.

'Why, thank you.' Von Berger accepted a light and leaned back, peering out at the crowded streets. 'Fascinating.'

'Yes, well, I think it will rain later.'

'Is that good?'

'In this city, yes. The smell can be overpowering and Baghdad was not created to fit in with the invention of the motor car. I'm taking you to the Al Bustan, Baron, a five-star modern hotel.'

'And my meeting?'

'He can't see you today. I'll let you know.'

'Of course.'

Already, von Berger was wondering whether he should have come in the first place.

Later that evening, he stood on the terrace of his suite, smoking a cigarette and drinking Irish whiskey. It was a strange thing to find in his suite and he wondered who had known enough about him to supply it. There was a flash of lightning and a rumble of thunder and rain started to pour down. He looked to the crowded streets, the slow-moving traffic, but already the air smelled fresher. It was as if a weight had been lifted. He finished his whiskey, and the mobile phone in his breast pocket, an international model, rang.

'Who is this?' he enquired.

'How about a drink in the Piano Bar?' said a woman's voice. 'Oh – sorry, that's not possible. You're at the Al Bustan in downtown Baghdad.'

He was astonished. 'Kate, it's you. Where are you?'

'Never mind.'

'And how on earth did you know I was here?'

'Oh, I know most things. That you're brokering some sort of arms deal with Saddam, for instance. When are you seeing him, or are you?'

'It was supposed to be today, but it's been delayed.'

'Who said so?'

'The young man who received me at the airport. A Major Aroun.'

'A major? They should be doing better than that for you. It all smells a little like old fish to me.'

'Well, dictators can be like that. I was raised on Hitler, remember.'

'All right, but listen, take care. I'll check back to see how you are. You'll be pleased to know we're making a fortune, partner.' The line went dead and he switched off.

He languished for three days, and had decided to go back home when the hotel phone finally rang. It was Aroun. 'He'll see you tonight at nine-thirty. I'll pick you up at nine and deliver you to the Presidential Palace.'

'How kind,' von Berger said. 'I was about to leave.'

'Please, Baron, his sense of humour is limited. In any case, you wouldn't have made the airport. I would suggest you be ready on time.'

Max von Berger laughed. 'My dear boy, I wouldn't miss it for anything.'

When von Berger went down to the hotel foyer in response to Aroun's phone call, he found the major standing by a Mercedes sedan. He wasn't in uniform and wore a black leather bomber jacket and jeans, as did the driver. Von Berger wore a black suit, white shirt and dark tie.

'I feel overdressed.'

'I was ordered to make this as low-key as possible. Get in.'

The Baron did, sitting in the rear, Aroun in front beside the driver. As they drove away, the thunder rumbled again and rain erupted, deluging the slow-moving traffic, a scene of chaos, horns honking, the sidewalks crowded with people, most of them seemingly oblivious to the rain.

'This is the main thoroughfare through the old town. Al Rashid Street. It's not too far to the palace.'

Al Rashid Street. It made von Berger think of Kate. She hadn't rung back. The car braked behind a truck close to the kerb, where several young men were sheltered under the awning of a café, smoking cigarettes and talking. As the Mercedes paused, they noticed it and stared, very much aware of von Berger's Western clothes. They began talking excitedly in Arabic, youths of a kind to be found in any great city in the world and intent on mischief. Suddenly, they approached the car, and someone wrenched open the rear door of the Mercedes.

'American, eh? We don't like Americans.'

'No, I'm German.'

'You lie – American.' Hands reached in for him.

Aroun got out on the other side and pulled a pistol, but three men jumped on him from behind, wrestled him to the

59

ground and started kicking him. His driver was dragged out and received the same treatment. Von Berger thought his last hour had come, as many hands grabbed at him, pulling him into the middle of the crowd. A tall, young, bearded man, incongruously in a baseball cap and T-shirt, seemed to be the leader. He brandished Aroun's pistol and shouted to the crowd, then advanced on von Berger as they held him.

'Americans we kill,' the man said.

But just then came a squeal of brakes, as two Land Rovers skidded to a halt, the sound of a shot fired into the air, and a woman calling in Arabic. The men turned, pulling von Berger with them, and he saw Kate Rashid standing by one of the Land Rovers in headcloth, khaki bush shirt and slacks. She was holding a Browning Hi-Power and the six Bedu guards with her had AK47s at the ready.

'Let him go,' she said in English to the man in the baseball cap.

'He is American and Americans we kill,' he shouted. 'And who are you, woman, to tell us what do?'

He grabbed von Berger by the hair and rammed the muzzle of his pistol against the Baron's skull. 'I say he dies.'

Her hand swung up, and she fired, shooting him through the mouth, the back of his skull fragmenting, blood and bone spraying over the crowd. He dropped the pistol and fell, and the crowd scattered and ran. The Baron had fallen to the ground and two of the Bedu picked him up.

'Kate,' he said, dumbfounded.

She smiled and turned to Aroun, who had picked himself up and leaned on the Mercedes. 'Major Aroun, I think you know who I am.'

'Yes, Lady Kate.'

'I don't know what's been going on here. No uniforms, no military escort?'

'He said it had to be low-profile.'

'Really? Well, you'd better see to the scum on the pavement, then clean yourself up, and I'll take the Baron to the Presidential Palace.' She turned to von Berger. 'Come on, get in and tidy yourself up. Your hair is all over the place.'

Sitting in the back of one of the Land Rovers as they drove away, he said, 'Where in the hell did you spring from?'

'Oh, I was in the region and heard a whisper relating to your meeting with the great man. For various reasons, I wasn't happy. Saddam can do strange things. He's a man of uncertainties. He sends a junior officer to greet you, leaves you kicking your heels for three days, a man as important as you? That means he's in another manic phase.'

'How do you know this?'

'Because I know him well. He's a good friend of mine. No, that's not quite right. He *thinks* he's a good friend of mine.'

'And you?'

'Oh, I think he's a madman who'd be better off dead. Achieving that would be difficult, however.'

They paused at the gates of the Presidential Palace, were checked through instantly when the guards saw Kate, and drove inside, stopping at the bottom of the huge steps leading up to the entrance.

Kate turned and said calmly, 'Well, here we go, Max. This should be interesting.'

An army colonel, who had presumably been waiting to greet the Baron, rushed forward to kiss Kate's hand and spoke to her in English.

'Lady Kate, I've heard what happened. It shames us all. Are you all right?'

It was so strange how English the Iraqi military sounded, the Baron thought. This was another one who'd probably gone to Sandhurst Military Academy.

61

'The only problem is the man I had to leave on the pavement, Colonel.'

'He was a dog who deserved to die for his insult to you. Pavements, Lady Kate, are easily cleaned.'

'Is he aware of what happened?'

'His rage was terrible. He has ordered instant police reprisals in Al Rashid Street. Please follow me.'

There was a sudden wailing of sirens outside, and the lights dimmed at once. The colonel waved a hand and a soldier ran forward with a large hand lamp.

'It's an air-raid practice only,' the colonel said. 'Our American friends are not giving us much trouble at the moment. This way.'

They followed him along corridors of marbled splendour. It was an eerie feeling, the darkness closing in, statues on each side seemingly floating out of the gloom, the pool of light from the lamp, the echo of their feet on the marble.

'Are you all right?' Kate whispered.

Von Berger said, 'I think you might say it's one of the more remarkable experiences I've ever had – and considering I'm the only man you know who was in the Führer Bunker, that's quite a statement.'

She laughed. 'Oh, I like you, Max. If only –'

'I was fifty years younger,' he cut in. 'But I'm not, so behave yourself.'

They halted at an ornate door, sentries on either side. The colonel opened it and went in. They waited and a voice rumbled. The colonel was back in a moment.

'He will see you now.'

Saddam Hussein was seated alone in uniform at a large desk, the only light a shaded lamp. He was signing documents, but looked up and put down his pen, got up and came round the desk to embrace her, kissed her on each cheek.

She said in English, 'Baron von Berger doesn't speak Arabic.'

Saddam never advertised the fact that he spoke English well, but he turned now. 'Baron, I'm outraged that you should be treated in such a fashion.'

'It was an unfortunate misunderstanding. They thought me an American. I think I was wearing the wrong clothes.'

Saddam roared with laughter. 'I like that. I can understand that.' It was strange how volatile he was, for just as suddenly he frowned and looked down at Kate, 'But the insult to you. That is unforgivable. I've ordered reprisals. The military police will teach the scum on Al Rashid Street a lesson.'

'But I did teach them a lesson,' Kate said. 'I shot the leader of the mob.'

'Excellent. That was *your* lesson and now I teach them *mine*. Come – sit.'

Which she did and nodded to von Berger, who took the next chair. Saddam passed across to a window and opened the shutters to a terrace. An 'All Clear' sounded and he looked across the city. Lights started to come on.

'We had the Americans and the Brits in the Gulf War, interfering, sticking their nose in Arab business. They fly over the so-called exclusion zones, bomb our installations. War, perhaps, will come again.' He turned, 'Which is why you are here, Baron.'

Max von Berger turned to Kate, and the look on her face said it all. He took a deep breath. 'In what way can I help?'

Kate cut in. 'Baron von Berger has access to most armaments. What are you looking for? Stinger missiles?'

He paced back into the room. 'That kind of thing I can get from many sources. What I really need is plutonium.' He turned to von Berger. 'My nuclear programme is well advanced, but we do need plutonium. Can you supply me?'

Kate turned and nodded slightly. Von Berger said, 'I am aware of sources.'

'Excellent.' Saddam sat behind his desk again. 'If the Americans come, at the end I must have a weapon, a special weapon to stop them dead in their tracks. People talk of biological weapons, but this is not enough. Only a nuclear device will suffice.'

Max von Berger could have pointed out the catastrophic results of American retaliation, cited the fate of Japan at the end of the Second World War, but didn't. There was no point. He now realized, at first hand, that Saddam Hussein was a madman.

'So, what do you want from me?' he asked.

'I told you. Plutonium, Baron, plutonium.' Saddam stood up and his head was shaking. 'Don't waste my time. Go away and get me plutonium.'

Von Berger was aware of Kate's hand on his arm and stood up. 'I'll see what I can do.'

Saddam picked up his pen and started to sign more documents. Kate pulled von Berger away and he had the good sense to go with her.

In the Land Rover, he said, 'He's a raving lunatic.'

'Of course, but that's not what's important now. I had my other Land Rover retrieve your belongings from the Al Bustan. I've also arranged a departure slot for your plane. You should get out while you can. His manic moods are terrible. You never know what he'll do.'

'I'll take your advice.'

'Will you try to find him plutonium?'

And Max von Berger, a major in the SS, once Hitler's aide, said, 'Not in a thousand years.'

'Good,' she said. 'You're a lovely man, Max, so let's get you to the airport and out of this place.'

GERMANY

4

It was the following year and von Berger was in Brazil on business when he heard of the appalling tragedy that had befallen the Rashid family, the deaths of the brothers George and Michael and Paul. The news came too late for him to fly back for the funeral, and what would have been the point?

Because of the particular nature of the peerage, Kate Rashid inherited, and was now Countess of Loch Dhu. But the rule still held: there was no public connection between the Baron and the Rashid empire.

At that stage, von Berger knew nothing of the reasons for the deaths or of the Rashid feud with Western interests or the cause for it. In time, he would hear of the failed assassination attempt on the life of President Jake Cazalet at his weekend retreat on Nantucket by Irish mercenaries, instigated by Paul Rashid. Then there was the successful assassination of the Sultan of Hazar himself, followed by the failed attempt on the lives of the entire Council of Elders in Hazar, again, by Irish mercenaries.

It was only later that von Berger realized how important in all this had been Blake Johnson, who ran the Basement at the White House. And then there was General Charles

Ferguson, who did the same thing for the British Prime Minister, seconded by his right-hand man, Sean Dillon. Dillon, who had personally killed Paul Rashid and his two brothers.

But all this knowledge was in the future. For the present, Max von Berger had to be content to follow Kate Rashid's activities from afar. He was aware of the arrival in her life of Rupert Dauncey, an American cousin of some kind, once a major in the Marine Corps, and was also aware of a certain jealousy. But life went on and he busied himself in business as usual, until that evening, staying for a few days at the Schloss, when on a whim, he decided to have supper at the inn, the Eagle.

It was crowded, a Friday night, snow falling, winter beginning. When he went in, he received his usual welcome, and the innkeeper, Meyer, hurried to meet him. 'Baron, are you dining with us tonight?'

'I think so. I'll take your special hotpot with potatoes and dumplings. How could I do better?'

'You honour us.'

He led the way to a booth in the far corner, and nodded to the two men sitting there, who jumped up and ducked their heads.

'Thank you, my friends.' The Baron took off his hat, and Meyer helped with the heavy coat and seated him. 'It's a bad night, so I'll have champagne. It'll liven things up a little.'

Meyer departed, and the Baron took out his case, selected a cigarette and lit it, aware of the man standing at the bar drinking beer and scowling at him. This was one Hans Klein, a huge brute, a local farmer and drunkard. He was seriously in arrears with his rent, had failed to pay again and again. At the town appeals court the previous month, the Baron had given him three months until eviction.

As Meyer brought the champagne in a bucket and a glass, Klein said loudly, 'That's all right for the high and bloody mighty.' He turned to the barmaid and slammed his hand on the bar. 'Schnapps, and be quick about it, or do we all have to stand in line for him?'

Conversation faltered and Meyer, thumbing off the cork, looked agitated. 'Baron, I'm so sorry.'

'Just pour.'

It was at that moment the door opened, snow whirled in, and the stranger appeared.

He was wearing a hunting jacket with a fur collar, and a tweed cap covered with snow, which he took off and beat against his thigh. Strangers were not usual in Neustadt and he attracted immediate attention. He had black hair, not quite to his shoulders, but long enough, and a handsome wedge-shaped face with a broken nose, with the look of some medieval brave about him. He unbuttoned his coat.

'Good evening,' he said. 'A bad night for it.'

His German was almost flawless, but as von Berger recognized, there was a hint of Italian there.

Meyer said, 'Welcome, mein Herr, you've come far?'

'You could say that. All the way from Sicily.'

Klein turned to those nearest him. 'Italian,' and there was contempt in his voice.

The stranger ignored him and said to Meyer, 'I need something to warm me up. You look as if you've got every drink in the world back there. Would you have grappa?'

'As a matter of fact, I do.' Meyer took a bottle down from the shelf and held it up.

The stranger read the label aloud, '"Grappa Di Brunella de Montalcino". Jesus, that stuff is firewater. Pour me one now.' He took it straight down and coughed. 'Wonderful. I'll hang on to it.'

He turned, saw a small table vacant, and in the same glance, the Baron in his booth, amused. The stranger stopped smiling and almost stepped back, as if recoiling physically. He paused, then went to the vacant table, sat down, opened the bottle and poured another one. He glanced at the Baron again, then lowered his eyes.

The Baron frowned, strangely uncomfortable. There was something familiar there. It was as if he knew him, but how could that be? Not that it mattered, for it was at that moment that Klein, drunker than ever, erupted. He reached over the bar, grabbed the bottle of schnapps, pulled the cork with his teeth and drank deeply, then he slammed the bottle down and turned.

'You think you're God Almighty, Baron, but I'll tell you what you are. You're a bastard.' He was so drunk he didn't know what he was saying. 'And I know how to treat bastards like you. Try to come on to my farm, I'll take my shotgun to you.'

There was total silence from everyone there. The Baron stayed quite calm, sat there, his hands folded over his cane.

'Go home, Klein, you are not yourself.'

Klein lurched forward and swept the champagne from the Baron's table. 'You old swine. I'll show you.'

'You'll show no one,' the stranger said, and poured another glass of grappa. 'And I suggest you apologize to a great man for insulting him so.'

The Baron glanced up at him, a slight frown on his face, and Klein turned, lurched across and leaned on the table. 'Italian pretty boy, eh? I'm going to break both your arms.'

'Really?' The stranger reversed his grip on the bottle and smacked it across the side of Klein's skull. The big man fell to one knee, and the stranger stood, picked up his chair, and smashed it across Klein's shoulders.

He backed away and Klein reached for the table and hauled himself up slowly. He turned, blood on his face, and the stranger said, 'You are an animal, my friend. Someone should have taught you this a long time ago.'

70

Klein roared with anger and staggered forward, the great hands reaching to destroy. The stranger swayed to one side, tripped him expertly, then kicked him in the side of the head. Klein rolled over, groaned and passed out.

There was an excited murmur and Meyer rushed from behind the bar. 'Baron, all this is terrible. What can I say?'

'Very little. Just get him to the police station. They can hold him in a cell overnight.'

Half-a-dozen men carried Klein out, while the crowd discussed the events excitedly, turning to look at the stranger, who watched as the barmaid brought a broom and cleared up. He poured another glass of grappa and drank it down in another single swallow. The girl went away.

The Baron said, 'You handle yourself well. Brutal and effective.'

'I was raised in Palermo.'

'You speak excellent German.'

'My mother raised me to.'

'I see. You looked at me as if you knew me.'

'Your photo, yes. I would have searched you out at the Schloss tomorrow. This meeting is by chance.'

'And to what purpose? We could start with your name.'

'Rossi – Marco Rossi. My mother was Maria Rossi. She was once in your employ.'

Max von Berger was aware of a slight trembling, a faintness. 'Sit down and give me some of that firewater.' Rossi filled the glass again and gave it to him and sat. 'Why are you here?'

'She died after a long fight with cancer. I was a captain in the Italian Air Force until six months ago. A Tornado pilot. I resigned so that I could be close to her. We lived with my uncle in Palermo, but he died a year ago, so she was alone.'

'But I don't understand. How can you be called Rossi?'

'Because my mother never married. She made me swear to bring her ashes to you, so here I am.' He took out a packet of cigarettes and the Baron said, 'I'll have one.' His hand shook as he accepted the light. 'That's better.' He pulled himself together. 'Why did she leave me? Do you know?'

'Oh, yes. She loved you deeply, but realized how much the memory of your wife remained with you, and I know that terrible story. When she found herself pregnant, she didn't want you to feel beholden or trapped in any way, so she went home to Palermo to the protection of my uncle, Tino Rossi. He was an important figure in the Mafia.'

'There was something about you when you came in, something familiar. It was as if I knew you,' the Baron said. 'Now I know why, but I can hardly take it all in. It's not every day a man finds he has a son. The same for you, I think.'

'Not exactly. I've known you were my father for the last twenty years.' Rossi stood up. 'I'll fix up a room here for tonight and bring the ashes in the morning, then I'm going home to see if the Air Force will take me back.'

'No, there's only one place you stay tonight, Schloss Adler. We must talk,' the Baron said, and he led the way out.

In the chapel at the Schloss, it was winter-cold and as always, the candles guttered and there was the smell of incense. The Baron had personally carried the casket with Maria Rossi's ashes and now he placed it in front of the family mausoleum.

'I will have her interred with my first wife and . . .' He broke then and sobbed deeply. 'Your brother.'

And Marco Rossi, the hard man, harder than even Max von Berger imagined at that time, was immensely moved, put an arm around him, held him close.

'It's all right, father, it's all right. Don't worry. I'm here. For this moment, I'm here. We mourn together. She loved you very much, believe me. She made a huge sacrifice for that love.'

Von Berger said, 'Because of me, my attitudes, my pride, the stupid von Berger seven-hundred-year-old pride.'

'Hey,' Marco said, 'that applies to me too, doesn't it?'

Von Berger wiped a tear from his eye and smiled. 'Quite true. Now let's go and perhaps have some supper, a drink, but most of all a chat.'

Later, in the Great Hall in front of a blazing log fire, the butler served coffee brandy.

'That's fine, Otto,' von Berger told him. 'We'll manage. You've made arrangements for Herr Rossi?'

'Yes, Baron, the Imperial Suite.'

'Fine. Good night.'

The butler disappeared into the gloom of the hall, footsteps echoing. Rossi said, 'Before anything else is said, I must tell you one thing.'

'And what is that?'

'As I told you, my uncle, Tino Rossi, was Mafia, but there's more to it than that. He was an important capo. You know what that means?'

'Of course.'

'When he died, he left my mother hugely wealthy, and with her death, that all comes to me. I need nothing from you. That's not why I'm here. I'm here for my mother and out of respect for my father. I know all about you. You were a great soldier and a great man.'

Von Berger waved it off. 'Tell me about yourself.'

'I spent my early years in Palermo, of course. Neither my mother nor my uncle wanted me in the Mafia, which was difficult, because all my extended family, my cousins, were.'

'Judging by the way you demolished a brute like Klein, they failed in their wishes.'

'I spent too much time as a boy on the Palermo streets. You learn fast there. I had a fine education, the best, but I suppose the Mafia was somehow in my blood. A kind of arrogance.' His hand came out of his pocket holding an ivory

Madonna; he pressed a button and a blade flashed. 'And this . . . I keep it always. My uncle gave it to me for my tenth birthday.' He folded it.

Von Berger said, 'So what came with maturity?'

'I was sent to Yale University at seventeen, studied economics, business. I did well enough, had a flair for computers. Then I went home and joined the Italian Air Force, and ended up getting shot down and on the run behind Serb lines in Bosnia.'

'That must have been difficult.'

'You could say that.'

'And you want to go back to it?'

'Why not? Within three months of qualifying, I was in the Gulf War, attacking Basra. Bosnia a few years later, Kosovo. It has a special feel, life on the edge. I don't have a girlfriend at the moment. A little action and passion wouldn't come amiss.'

'I can understand that. Pour me another brandy.'

Marco did so, lit a cigarette and said calmly, 'As I've said, I didn't come to seek any advantage from you. In your position, however, I'd be wanting a DNA test.'

'And that might be a good idea,' the Baron said. 'But only for one reason – to secure the line, to legitimize you. You're quite obviously my son. I have no dispute with it; in fact, I welcome it. I only dispute this nonsense of you returning to the Air Force. You've taken the pitcher to the well far too often. Enough is enough.'

'So what do I do?'

'You've got a first-class business background, you're a war hero, and it appears you're a rather ruthless young man if someone crosses you. A street fighter.'

'What did my father do to the Ukrainians who butchered his wife and my half-brother? I come from a long line of warriors.'

'Exactly, which is why I wish you to choose to stay with me. To be my right hand.' The Baron shook his head. 'Dammit,

I'll be eighty next year and to have my son beside me would be such a benison. I realize you are wealthy and . . .'

Marco Rossi, filled with an emotion he had only experienced with his mother, said, 'No – please.' He dropped to one knee, took the Baron's hand and kissed it. 'You have no idea what this means. To be the son of a man like you.'

'But I do.' Von Berger put a hand to Marco's head. 'Because I am the father of a man like you.'

And Marco took to his new position in life like a duck to water. From then on, wherever the Baron went, so did he. It became common knowledge that he was, in fact, von Berger's son.

And in intimate moments, the Baron told him everything. About the Führer Bunker and the last interview with Hitler and the source of his enormous wealth; he even told him of the Hitler diary and showed him where he kept it, the secret compartment at the back of the mausoleum with the eternal flame burning in an open bowl. Yet he never let him read it – the secret of Hitler's overtures to Roosevelt to end the Second World War was von Berger's alone.

He explained the special and secret relationship with Rashid Investments, how Kate Rashid had saved his life, his blood bond with her. All this, Marco took on board and understood. And then came that dreadful morning in his suite at the Grand Hotel in Berlin, sitting down to breakfast, when Marco joined him and handed him the early copy of *The Times*.

'I think you'd better read this.'

It was a front-page account of Kate Rashid's final tragic flight from Dauncey Place. Max von Berger had seldom felt such anguish. He slammed a hand on the table.

'But what went wrong, for God's sake? She was a fine pilot.'

'No one knows. Engine failure, probably. I did some NATO training there with the RAF. I know that coast. Sussex, the marshes, the mudflats, then that damned English weather. From the report, it was a dawn flight, with mist and rain, and according to air traffic control, her plane was on the screen for a short while, then vanished. As you can see, they've begun searching off the coast.' Marco went to the bar, poured a brandy and brought it to him. 'Drink it down.'

The Baron did as he was told. 'I owed her so much. My very life.'

Marco felt strangely detached, in a way almost jealous. He lit two cigarettes and passed one to his father. 'She must have gone down close in. That means reasonably shallow water. They'll find her, and this cousin you told me about, Rupert Dauncey.'

'Yes, I suppose so.' He held out his glass. 'I'd better have another.'

Marco went and got it and brought it back. 'What happens now?'

Von Berger had not even thought of it until now. 'The legal agreements with Paul Rashid passed to Kate, and now, on her death, they will come into force for me. I will assume control of the Rashid empire.' He took a deep breath, stunned. He had never actually considered it, not with four Rashids so vital and healthy. 'We must alert our people in Geneva, here in Berlin, London. Everything must be put into motion.'

'They've still got to find her body. That will take time. Then there needs to be a pathologist's report, a coroner's inquest.'

The old man, strangely tranquil, said, 'Yes, of course, but we must begin now. There will be no need for secrecy any longer. I'll speak to the chief executives of Rashid in New York and London, so they know what to expect. They'll come to heel. They will have no option.'

'And me? What do you want me to do?'

'Ah, for you I have a special task. You will take over all of the security operations for Rashid worldwide. There was

76

a lot going on there, particularly in Arabia and Hazar, and I want to know what it was. How did the three Rashid brothers come to die, and why, and now Kate? It's a remarkable coincidence.'

'Whatever you say.'

'You're a genius with a computer, Marco, and you'll be able to access everything they have. You'll have the authority.'

'London first?'

'I suppose so. I'll speak to the Rashid people there, then New York. By that time, they'll have either found her or declared her dead.'

'Can I do anything for you?'

'Arrange for the Gulfstream to London Northolt.'

'I'll get on it.'

He went out, and Max von Berger sat there, thinking. Life, he thought, was always so unexpected, one different journey after another, and this one, he told himself with a heavy heart, was to end in only one place. In the churchyard of the village of Dauncey.

LONDON
THE PRESENT

5

The church door opened and the cortège appeared, the Baron and Marco close behind. The procession started through the graveyard to the family mausoleum.

'Come on,' Ferguson said, 'I want to see this.'

The coffin was on a central dais and people walked around it slowly, paying their respects. The lid was half-open, the embalmed body of Kate Rashid revealed. The Baron reached it and paused, then he took something from his pocket, leaned forward and placed it on her breast. He moved forward, paused to glance at Ferguson, then continued.

Dillon whispered, 'What in the hell was that about?'

They took their turn by the coffin, gazing down at Kate Rashid's calm dead face, remarkably lifelike, thanks to the embalmer's art. Dillon felt no emotion, or told himself he didn't. What the Baron had left was a medal, scarlet and black, the German cross. They moved on.

'How interesting,' Ferguson observed. 'He's awarded her his Knight's Cross with Oak Leaves and Swords. There's far more here than even we know about.'

Everyone started to turn away through the rain. Dillon

said, 'Where is this leading, Charles?'

'To the Dauncey Arms, Dillon. I understand that there will be a champagne buffet there.'

'And Baron Max von Berger?' Blake asked.

'Well, let's go and see,' Ferguson told him and led the way.

The Dauncey Arms was already filling up, as people filtered into the saloon bar. Like everything else in the village, it was ancient: black beams on the ceiling, a log fire burning on the old granite fireplace. There were tables in oak booths. Blake managed to grab one and eased in with Ferguson. Dillon moved to the bar, where Betty Moody, the landlady, presided.

She frowned. 'I didn't know you'd be coming, Mr Dillon. You're not welcome here.'

'I'm not welcome anywhere, Betty.' Dillon took a glass of champagne from the row on the bar, swallowed it down, took three more and went back to the booth. 'There you go.' He gave Ferguson and Blake a glass each and toasted them.

Blake said, 'Even you don't know this, General, but not more than twenty-four hours ago, the Baron sought and received a meeting in the Oval Office with the President. I was there. He told him that he was now in control of Rashid Investments, and, most importantly, Rashid Oil. A third of all Middle East oil production. He wanted concessions – and the President pointed out that he wasn't comfortable with that.'

'Why?' Dillon said.

'Because Berger has been dealing with Iraq on arms deals. We can't stop the oil production – the world market needs it – but the President made it clear that he was not welcome.'

'How sad,' Ferguson said. 'He's seeing the Prime Minister tomorrow morning.'

'And what will happen there?' Dillon asked.

'The same answer, I expect.'

'Has the PM spoken to you?'

'Briefly, on the phone. He's asked me to attend the meeting.' He shrugged. 'It's a foregone conclusion.'

It was at that moment that the Baron and Marco Rossi entered the bar. The Baron glanced around, saw them and came across. His voice was deep, quite pleasant, with only a hint of a German accent.

'Ah, Mr Johnson. Nice to see you again.'

Blake didn't stand. 'Baron.'

'General Ferguson.' Berger nodded. 'We haven't met.'

'We will tomorrow at Downing Street.'

'Really?' Von Berger smiled. 'I look forward to it. Your reputation precedes you.'

'It usually does.'

The Baron turned to Dillon. 'And you must be the great Sean Dillon – a remarkable man.'

'Jesus, Baron,' Dillon said. 'And what would you be after?'

'Your head, of course. Kate Rashid was my dear friend. She even saved my life once. So – I'll settle for your head.'

Dillon replied in German. 'You can always try.'

There was a frozen moment, and Ferguson said, 'I really wouldn't bother with Downing Street tomorrow if I were you, Baron.'

'I always travel hopefully, General. Good day to you, gentlemen.'

Rossi eyed Dillon, his face hard, watchful.

'Go on, son, our day will come.'

Rossi smiled as if in satisfaction, turned and followed the Baron out.

Ferguson said, 'So what do you think?'

'Kate Rashid was a dear friend, even saved his life, and all he wants is my head?' Dillon shrugged. 'We've got trouble here, Charles, big trouble.'

'I'm afraid you're right.' He turned to Blake. 'What about you?'

'The President has asked the Prime Minister to allow me to attend your meeting, too. After that, I'll return to Washington.'

'Excellent. We might as well get back to London.' Ferguson turned to Dillon. 'You've got your final debriefing this evening.'

'Debriefing, my arse,' Dillon said, and smiled at Blake. 'He's got me into psychoanalysis now after my last little run-in with friend Rashid. Obviously has me down as some kind of psychotic.'

There was an edge to him, which Blake sensed. 'Routine, Sean, routine. You went through a lot, had to kill more than once.'

'Really?' Dillon said. 'I thought I killed everybody. Still – back to London and the Mother Superior.'

He started for the door. Blake said, 'Mother Superior?'

'One of Dillon's bad jokes. The person he's seeing is a friend of mine, a lady called Haden-Taylor. She's not only a psychiatrist, but a professor and an ordained priest of the Church of England. She operates out of Harley Street – or St Paul's Church, around the corner, if you can't afford to pay.'

'I see. She's like that, is she?'

'Very much so.'

'Ah well,' Blake said as he followed him out. 'It takes all sorts, I suppose.'

In the rear of the Rolls-Royce, the Baron said to Rossi, 'It's nice to put a face to Ferguson and Dillon. Computer printouts lack charm.'

'A hard one, the Irishman,' Rossi said. 'What I've already seen on the Rashid computer is bad. There's no doubt he killed all three Rashid brothers.'

'Yes, well, my impression is they asked for it.' The Baron shook his head. 'That attempt on Cazalet's life on Nantucket was ill-advised. You only do a thing like that if you're certain you can succeed. Failure only brings disaster.'

'The Irish mercenaries were well recommended,' Rossi said.

'And well taken care of by Dillon and company.' Max von Berger shook his head. 'But we still don't know for absolute certainty if they were responsible for Kate's death. I want you to keep on scouring those security files at Rashid Investments for any kind of clue. There must be something there.'

'Don't worry, I will. I have come across something, actually. The names of two guys who worked directly for Rashid Security under Rupert Dauncey's orders. They were ex-SAS, named Newton and Cook. They were definitely involved in watching Dillon.'

'Do you know where they are now?'

'Working for a third-rate security firm. I'm meeting them later this afternoon.'

The Baron frowned. 'Be careful, Marco. Maybe you should take some muscle.'

'Not for these two.' Rossi smiled coldly. 'I'm muscle enough.'

The old man paused. 'You mean a great deal to me.'

'I know that.'

'And this Dillon is bad news. Did you notice his eyes? Like water over a stone. No expression.'

'Not surprising, given his background. All those years with the IRA, all the killings, and the Brits never managed to lay a hand on him.' Marco smiled. 'Until Ferguson shopped him to the Serbs, then, in a manner of speaking, bought him back, blackmailed him into working for him.'

The old man said, 'This rumour that he tried to blow up the Prime Minister and the War Cabinet in ninety-one. You think it's true?'

'Oh, yes, and it made him rich. He was paid a fortune by the Iraqis. Money means nothing to him.'

'A warrior, a soldier, just like you, Marco.'

'And you, Baron.'

'A long time ago.' The old man smiled. 'Now give me a cigarette, and don't tell me I shouldn't.'

The Grenadier was a first-class pub much frequented by Guards officers, an opulent Victorian sort of place, with an impressive mahogany bar and booths where one could eat well on traditional English food. At that time in the afternoon, it was quiet when Marco walked in. He stood there looking around, his trench coat damp, a briefcase in one hand, then recognized Newton and Cook from their computer photos and approached.

'I'm Rossi.'

They were what he'd expected, big men in their mid-forties, once solid, now fleshing out, in bad suits.

They looked at him, carefully showing nothing. 'What can we do for you? Want a drink?' Cook asked.

Rossi took off his coat and waved to the bar. 'A large vodka martini and two large Scotches.' He sat down and didn't smile when he said, 'Trust me. You're going to need them.'

Newton said, 'What is this?'

'Shut up. You used to work for Rupert Dauncey at Rashid and now you work for a shit company – I can't even remember the name – so I ask the questions.'

Cook looked sullen, but said nothing.

'Dauncey gave you orders to follow a guy named Sean Dillon. I'd like to know what those orders were.'

'Is Dillon in this?' Newton asked.

'Would that matter?'

Cook said, 'He kills people, that bastard.'

'And it bothers you?'

'It would bother anyone with sense.'

Marco nodded. 'All right, how's this for sense?' He pushed the briefcase over. 'There's five grand in there. You were dogging Dillon just after he returned to London from Hazar. If you want what's in there – start talking.'

Newton said, 'We heard the whispers. They were going to blow up a railway bridge in Hazar, the Rashids. Dillon fucked them up, along with a pal of his.'

'And who would that be?'

'Billy Salter, a well-known gangster. His uncle, Harry, has been one of the most important guvnors in the East End for years. Gone legit now – supposedly. He's big in property development by the Thames. They're very thick with Dillon.'

'So it would seem.'

'The thing is, the Rashids got their hands on Billy at the end of that business in Hazar. Kate Rashid went crazy. Shot Salter a few times. In the back, if you follow me.'

'And Dillon wasn't pleased?'

'No, and neither was the Countess. Dauncey told us she wanted us to jump him in London, sling him in the back of the van and drive him down to Dauncey Place to take care of him proper.'

'And this was when?'

'The night before she flew off in that plane.'

Marco nodded. 'Let me guess. Dillon got the drop on you?'

'That's right,' Cook said.

'Taunted us, really,' Newton said. 'Told us to tell Dauncey he'd be seeing him soon.'

'And did you?'

'Yes I did, and not because I'd much time for Dauncey. It was just that I liked to think he might be able to sort Dillon out if he appeared.'

'So Dillon probably turned up in the early hours of the morning when she flew out.'

'I'd say so.'

'It didn't occur to you to notify the police of any of this after you read about the crash?'

'You've got to be joking,' Newton said. 'Whatever went on here wasn't the kind of thing we wanted to get involved with.'

'All right. Anything else?'

'That's it.'

Marco pushed the briefcase a little closer. 'Then this is yours.' He stood and pulled on his trench coat. 'Nine o'clock, Monday morning, report to the Rashid security division. Ask for Taylor. I'll tell him to expect you.'

Newton looked at Cook, uncertain. 'I'm not so sure. I mean, Dillon . . .'

'Leave Dillon to me. On the other hand, if you'd rather stay working as bouncers at some third-rate night club, feel free.'

Newton stood up and said hurriedly, 'No, we're with you, Mr Rossi.'

Which bound them to him and suited him perfectly.

'In fact, you could take the rest of the day off and do me a favour. Dillon has a cottage in a place called Stable Mews.'

Newton glanced at Cook. 'Yes, we know it.'

'Hang around outside. See where he goes. Follow him.' He took out a card. 'My mobile number is on that. If there's anything interesting, give me a call.'

Within fifteen minutes of arriving at Stable Mews, Newton and Cook saw Dillon drive out of the garage in a Mini Cooper and followed him. Twenty minutes later, they reached Harley Street and saw Dillon park, walk up steps to a door with a brass plate beside it and go in.

'I'll have a look,' Newton said.

He checked the plate, frowned and came back to the car, then called Rossi on his mobile. 'It says Professor the Reverend Susan Haden-Taylor, Clinical Psychiatrist.'

'And he's still in there?'

'Yes.'

'I'll come straight around.'

A moment later, Dillon emerged, but didn't return to his car. Instead, he went down the street, turned the corner and crossed the road to a church. Newton saw him go inside, paused, then crossed the road himself. He phoned Rossi, who was in his car.

'He's gone round the corner to a church called St Paul's, and get this – the priest's name on the noticeboard is the same as the psychiatrist's.'

'I'll be with you in a few minutes,' Rossi told him and switched off.

Now what in the hell was Dillon up to?

The church was Victorian and smelled of damp, also of burning candles and incense. It was a dark and secret place, only the altar glowing in candlelight, a statue of the Virgin and Child to one side. It was old-fashioned Church of England, but it always took Dillon back to his Roman Catholic childhood and the Jesuits who'd had a hand in his education.

'Remember, wee Sean,' he said. 'One corruption is all corruption. By the small things shalt thou know them.' And how many times had that helped him over the years? Of course, in the end, it meant you didn't trust anybody.

The vestry door was closed. He listened to the murmur of voices, sighed and sat in one of the pews, thinking of Kate Rashid. 'Two churches in one day, old son. This could get to be a habit.'

Behind him, Marco Rossi slipped in cautiously through the open door, saw him, faded into the darkness at the rear and sank on to a rush-bottomed chair behind a pillar in the corner. After a while the vestry door opened and a young girl emerged, crying a little. Professor Susan Haden-Taylor was with her, a calm, pleasant woman in a clerical collar and a cassock. She put an arm round the girl, who was carrying a bag.

'Off you go, Mary. They're expecting you. St Paul's Hospice, Sloane Street. Stay as long as you like. We'll sort it out together. God bless.'

'And God bless you, Reverend.'

The girl moved out. Professor Haden-Taylor didn't notice Dillon in the gloom of the other side of the aisle, picked up a broom from somewhere, went to the altar and started to sweep the floor.

'If it's not one thing, it's another with you,' Dillon said. 'Comforting the weak and then brushing the bloody floor.'

She paused, turned and saw him. 'Seventeen, Sean, that's all, and with no one to help her. And she's not weak. She's just been diagnosed with breast cancer.'

'God dammit,' he exploded. 'Me and my big mouth.'

'It's your nature,' she said calmly.

'God, I feel rotten. Can I help? Could I give you a cheque?'

'Easily done, Sean. After all, you're a rich man. All that money for a wicked deed. Trying to see off the Prime Minister . . .' She smiled like an angel. 'But I'll take the cheque. The hospice needs to have the central heating refurbished and some plumbing work in the kitchen.'

'It's the hard woman you are, but it's a deal.'

'Excellent.' She sat in a pew two rows away, facing him. 'Not that it will do your immortal soul much good, mark you. You can have a cigarette if you want. God won't mind.'

'The decent ould stick he is.' Dillon lit up. 'So now what? A final debriefing, Ferguson said. I thought I'd covered everything.'

'I just want you to cover it again.'

'Why?'

'It's called catharsis, Sean. A kind of mental outpouring which could be good for you. That's an unlocking of things you've been turning away from.'

'Like all those years with the IRA? All the killing? You've got to be joking.'

'All right. Your conflict with the Rashids. You killed all three brothers.'

'Who were trying to kill me.'

'You ruined Kate Rashid's plans and she tried to kill Billy Salter. You came back to London angry and she tried to have you kidnapped.'

'You've heard all this.'

'And I want to hear it again. Tell me everything.'

'All right. I told the guys I jumped to tell Rupert Dauncey I'd be calling in at Dauncey Place in the early hours of the morning.'

'How did you feel?'

'Well, I armed myself to the teeth and drove down from London. Ferguson hadn't ordered it. This was me.' He lit another cigarette and drifted into the past. 'I liked Kate Rashid, always did, but she was barking mad, responsible for too much blood, and Billy was the last straw.' In a way he ignored her, thinking back. 'I always told myself that the IRA, all the killing, was because my father was killed in the crossfire of a firefight between Provos and Brit paratroopers in Belfast, but driving down that morning, in the darkness and rain, I remembered one of my favourite philosophers, Heidegger. For authentic living, he said, what is necessary is the resolute confrontation of death. So what if, for me, it's been a mad game, constantly seeking death? Any psychiatrist worth their salt could have come up with that one.'

'Did you believe that?'

He smiled. 'Not really. Only as a motivation.'

'So what happened at the house?'

'I already told you. I let Rupert get the drop on me. Why? Because I think I was a little mad, too, that morning. A death wish. I was on the edge, and she'd gone way over the edge. She had the Black Eagle on her private landing strip, so Rupert tied my hands, we got on board and took off. She made it clear he was going to throw me out at three thousand feet. I had a knife in my boot and cut myself free.'

'And?'

'Rupert dropped the Airstair door. I had a small Colt in an ankle holster. Full of surprises, me. I shot him in the head and pushed him out.'

'And she?'

'Went right over. Said we'd go to hell together. The Black Eagle has an ignition key. She switched off and threw the key out. I took over the control and made an engineless water landing. Unfortunately, she had a gun in her purse and tried to shoot me. I managed to jump out with the dinghy and she went down with the plane.' He shrugged. 'But you know all this.'

'Do you feel any different now?'

'Absolutely not.'

'What would you say was the worst moment?'

He frowned. 'Two, I suppose. Being swept in on the Sussex Bore at such speed in the dinghy, and then finding Rupert Dauncey's body alongside, all the way into the estuary marsh. We grounded at the old abandoned pier at Marsham.'

'Which was when you called Ferguson?'

'I had my mobile with me. I filled him in.'

'And what did he do?'

'Came down with the disposal team from London. I sat under the pier for three hours in the rain and waited.'

'The disposal team?'

'From the crematorium we use in North London. Rupert Dauncey became eight pounds of grey ash very quickly.'

'Did that bother you?'

'Not really. He was responsible for many things, but the death of the young daughter of a friend particularly damned him.'

'And Kate Rashid?'

'I'd seen the GPS as we went down in the sea, so I knew where she was. Ferguson gave the job to the Royal Marine Special Boat Squadron. We went in an old fishing boat.'

'You chose to go?'

'That's right. Found her in the cabin at ninety feet.'

'You saw her?'

'I pulled her out. Went up with her on the line. You have to do that slowly from ninety feet.'

'It must have been quite an experience.'

'You could say that.' He lit another cigarette. 'Going through it all again, has it helped? I don't feel particularly cathartic. What's that make me? Psychotic?'

She said calmly. 'There's a quotation: There are men of a rough persuasion who are willing to take care of the kinds of situations that ordinary people can't. They're called soldiers.'

'I know that one, and you couldn't have paid me a greater compliment. If that's all, I'll be on my way. Thanks, love.'

'Take care, Dillon.'

He turned away, paused and turned back. 'Look, sometimes I get this dream. I'm going down to the plane and I reach it and hang on and look inside and she isn't there. Does that make any kind of sense?'

'Perfectly.' She shook her head. 'My poor Dillon, such a good man in spite of everything, and yet you are what you are.'

'You're a great comfort.'

'Watch your back, my friend, isn't that what they say in Belfast?'

He left and she turned, went up to the altar and knelt in prayer. Behind her, Marco Rossi tiptoed out.

The Baron was using the Rashid house in South Audley Street not far from Park Lane. He sat by the fire in the Georgian living room and listened intently. When Marco was finished, the old man took a deep breath.

'Get me a brandy, Marco. We always suspected this, but it's still a shock.'

Marco went and got the drink, gave it to him and offered a cigarette from a silver case. 'So what do you want me to do?'

'Nothing yet. We'll see what the Prime Minister has to say tomorrow.'

'And then?'

'Marco, you didn't meet Kate Rashid. It was just before you came into my life, and our business dealings, of their very nature, had to be private, but one thing is a fact. I am only sitting here now because of her. I can only pay her back in one way. What she failed to achieve, I will achieve for her.'

Marco looked taken aback. 'What? You don't mean – Cazalet?'

'Oh, I have something in mind for the President, all right, but we'll take it slowly. Ferguson and Dillon come first. Yes, first, we'll deal with them. I'm sure you'll be up for that, Marco, won't you?'

At Downing Street the following morning, the Baron and Marco Rossi were admitted and shown to the Cabinet Room, where they found Ferguson and Blake Johnson waiting, standing on either side of the Prime Minister, who sat in his usual centre chair.

'Baron,' he said. 'Please be seated. This won't take long.'

The Baron sat and Rossi stood behind him. 'I appreciate your frankness. What is the problem, Prime Minister?'

'Berger International was already giving us problems. Your dealings with Iraq, for example, are not acceptable.'

'It's a free market.'

'Not when it comes to arms dealing. Now we hear of your connection with Rashid and your control over the oil market. It won't do, not in the context of terrorism, and the Middle East and Southern Arabia. To be frank, my government will place every obstacle we can think of in your way.'

'Excellent,' the Baron stood up. 'So now we know where we stand. Good morning, Prime Minister,' and he walked out, followed by Rossi.

The Prime Minister turned to Ferguson. 'Keep an eye on him, General. I don't trust that man one bit.'

Outside Number Ten, the Baron was still sitting in his Rolls-Royce, the door open, Rossi standing beside it, as Ferguson approached.

'Was there something else, Baron?'

'Don't bother with your disposal team, General, I'm not Rupert Dauncey.'

'Oh, dear, I'm afraid I don't know what you're talking about,' Ferguson said.

'Don't bother. I know everything.'

'So what does that mean?'

'It means that I am declaring *jihad* on you in memory of my dear friend Kate Rashid. Tell that to Dillon, and the rest of your friends.'

Rossi joined him, closed the door and they drove away.

'Well, to quote our hostile friend, at least now we know where we stand, Charles.' Blake shook hands. 'I'll see you.'

Ferguson went to his Daimler, the chauffeur standing beside it. Dillon was waiting in the rear and Ferguson joined him. He punched a number on his mobile. It was answered instantly.

'Who is this?'

'Roper, this is Ferguson. Get yourself down to the Dark Man and bring the file you've prepared on von Berger. We've got problems.'

'Will Sean be with you?'

'Yes.'

'On my way.'

As they drove off, Dillon said, 'Well?'

'Oh, the Prime Minister put the boot in hard. No kind of government co-operation. They'll place all sorts of obstacles in the Baron's way.'

'And how did he take it?'

'He's just declared *jihad* on all of us in memory of Kate Rashid – and he told me he wasn't a candidate for the disposal team.'

'That's interesting.'

'He knows, Dillon, God knows how. So I think it's time we had a council of war.'

'Well, that makes sense.' Dillon lit a cigarette. 'Quite like old times.'

As they progressed through the usual bad London traffic, Dillon thought about Berger and what he would entail. The Daimler turned along a narrow lane between warehouse developments and came out on a wharf beside the Thames. They parked outside the Dark Man, Salter's pub, its painted sign showing a sinister individual in a dark cloak.

The main bar was very Victorian: mirrors, mahogany bars behind, porcelain beer pumps. Dora, the barmaid, sat on a stool reading the *Evening Standard*.

The afternoon trade was light except for four men in the corner booth, and a fifth alongside. Harry Salter, his nephew Billy, his minders, Joe Baxter and Sam Hall, and Major Roper in his wheelchair.

Harry Salter looked up, saw Dillon first. 'You little Irish bastard. And you, General. What's going on?'

'Oh, a great deal, Harry.' Ferguson squeezed in. 'We've got trouble and it affects all of us. How are you, Roper?'

The man in the state-of-the-art wheelchair smiled. He wore a reefer coat, his hair down to his shoulders, and his face was a taut mass of the scar tissue associated with burns. A Royal Engineers bomb disposal expert, decorated with the George Cross, his extraordinary career had been terminated by what he called a 'silly little bomb' in a family car in Belfast.

He'd survived and discovered a whole new career in computers. Now, if you wanted to find out anything in cyberspace, it was Roper you called.

'I'm fine, General.'

'And you have the file?'

'Yes.'

'Good. Excellent.'

'Here, what goes on?' Harry Salter asked.

Ferguson said, 'You see to the drinks, Dillon, and I'll fill them in.'

Afterwards, Harry Salter said, 'So we're back with Kate Rashid. She was going to knock us all off, and now *this* geezer has taken over.'

Dillon, standing at the bar, was joined by Billy, who said, 'What do you think, Dillon?'

'I think he's serious business, Billy.'

'Well, we've handled serious business before.'

'Yes, and it got you a bullet through your neck, eighteen stitches in your face and two bullets through the pelvis.'

'Dillon, I'm fit now. I work with a personal trainer every day.'

'Billy, you jumped out of an aeroplane for me at four hundred feet, twice. It's over, that kind of thing.'

'So, I'm still good on the street.'

'We'll see, younger brother.'

Behind them, Ferguson had finished. Harry Salter said, 'A right bastard, this one. Just as bad as her.'

'So it would appear. What do you think, Roper?'

'Well, the coming together of Rashid and Berger does make them one of the most powerful corporations in the world. It's the apotheosis of capitalism – if that doesn't sound too Marxist.'

Ferguson nodded. 'It's like a bad novel, the whole thing.' He turned to Harry Salter. 'I've had a trying morning, Harry. Could I have your famous shepherd's pie and an indifferent red wine? I'm in need of comfort.'

6

At the Rashid house in South Audley Street the Baron sat in the drawing room with Marco.

'So what's our game plan?' Marco asked.

'Let's start by taking some action against the small fry, these gangsters, the Salters.'

'I'll work something out. I have Newton and Cook keeping Dillon's place under surveillance.'

'Any particular reason?'

'Just to keep an eye on him, see where he goes, what contacts he makes. I've given Newton the addresses of those involved on a regular basis with him, also computer photos.'

'Where did you get those?'

'From the computer right here in the study. There's a mass of information there – details of various schemes and operations Kate Rashid had put into play.'

'Business?'

'Of a sort.'

'I'll leave it all to you, for the moment, Marco. With the merger of the two companies, I have enough on my hands. Just keep me informed.'

'Of course, Father,' Marco said and went out.

The next morning, the 'council of war' had moved to Roper's apartment in Regency Square. It was on the ground floor, with its own entrance and a slope to aid wheelchair users. Roper insisted on looking after himself and had had the apartment, from bathroom to kitchen, specially designed to take care of his problems.

His sitting room had been turned into a state-of-the-art computer laboratory, including some highly classified equipment, which was there mainly because it suited Charles Ferguson. Over the years since his disaster in Belfast, Roper had become a legend in the world of computers. He had broken every kind of system from Moscow to Washington and he had proved his worth to Ferguson and the Prime Minister on more than one occasion.

On that morning, Sean Dillon arrived first in his Mini Cooper, parked and pressed the doorbell. The voice box crackled and Roper said, 'Who is it?'

'Sean, you idiot, let me in.'

The door swung open and he went through into the sitting room and found Roper in his wheelchair at the bank of computers. He crossed to a sideboard, found a bottle of Irish whiskey and poured one.

'Paddy? OK, well, it's not Bushmills, but you're improving.'

'I'm on a pension, Dillon. The Ministry of Defence being as parsimonious as it is, I have to watch my pennies.'

'You could always sell your medals. The Military Cross would do okay, but the George Cross would make a fortune.'

'You're always so amusing.' Roper tried a smile, always difficult with that ravaged, burned face.

'Don't start feeling sorry for yourself. Ferguson said you had found something?'

'Yes, but let's wait for them.' The front doorbell went and he pressed the remote control. 'Here they are.'

A moment later, Ferguson appeared, and with him, a woman in her late thirties, with red hair, wearing an Armani trouser suit. She looked like some high-level business executive, but she was Ferguson's assistant, Detective Superintendent Hannah Bernstein, on loan to him from Special Branch. She had an MA in Psychology from Oxford, but she had killed more than once in the line of duty.

'Ah, Dillon,' the general said, 'we can get straight on with it. What have you got for us, Major?'

'You wanted me to have a look at von Berger in general, the way he's been able to take over Rashid? Well, I discovered something interesting. A couple of years ago, he hiked two billion into Rashid for their oil exploration in Hazar and the Empty Quarter.'

There was silence. Hannah said, 'Where on earth would he get that sort of money?'

'Swiss banks. And it made me smell a rather large rat.'

It was Dillon who said, 'Let me guess. We're into Nazi gold.'

'And not only that,' said Roper. 'I got this story from an Israeli intelligence source. Von Berger was in Baghdad to see Saddam on some arms deal – and he was attacked by a mob in the old city. They were going to lynch him, when Kate Rashid came on the scene with a few Bedus, pistol in hand, and saved his life.'

'I can see it now,' Dillon said.

'Not being able to sleep at two-thirty in the morning, as often happens,' Roper went on, 'I decided to go back even farther on von Berger. You know that story that he left Berlin in a Storch that happened to be there as a back-up in case von Greim's Arado had problems? He told American and British intelligence that it was simply opportunistic. He knew it was waiting in Goebbels' garage and commandeered it.'

'Only you don't buy it,' Dillon put in.

'Not for a moment. It was all too convenient. So I decided to access the Führer Bunker on my computer. I worked through

100

the Records Office, the accounts of his interrogations, then I got into the University of Berlin's stuff on the Bunker, all the people there, those who died, those who faded away, those who rushed into the night in a mostly vain attempt to escape the Russians. Von Berger's escape was obviously logged.'

'Where is this getting us?' Hannah asked.

'They've kept their records updated. Would you like to know how many people who were in the Führer Bunker in nineteen forty-five are still in the land of the living now?'

Ferguson said, 'Other than eighty-year-old Max von Berger?'

'Yes. How would you like Sara Hesser, an SS auxiliary, who was used by the Führer as a relief secretary for his last six months in the Bunker? She was twenty-two years old in April, nineteen forty-five. That makes her seventy-nine now.'

'Jesus,' Dillon said.

Ferguson said, 'You're obviously leading up to something.'

'Yes, you could say that. In the final debacle, when everyone fled the Bunker, by some miracle she was one of those who got through the underground tunnels and finally reached the West. She was in the hands of British intelligence in Munich, interrogated and released. In nineteen forty-five, she met a British captain called George Grant, who was serving in the army of occupation. He married her two years later.'

'And what happened?' Hannah demanded.

'She came to England. He was a lawyer. They never had children. According to her interrogation reports, she'd been gang-raped by Russian soldiers.'

'My God,' Hannah said. 'And now?'

'Her husband died of cancer five years ago. She lives at twenty-three Brickfield Lane, that's in Wapping by the Thames. You can extract anything from these things.' He tapped the computer. 'It's a three-storied terrace house that she and her husband owned for forty-five years. The way London property has gone these days, it's worth nine hundred thousand.'

'I think that deserves another drink.' Dillon went to the Paddy bottle.

Ferguson said, 'You're telling us that we have a woman who was a secretary to Hitler in the last few months of the war?'

'Oh, yes. Marrying an English officer and all that, she just got lost, I suppose.'

'And she would have known von Berger, must have known him,' said Dillon.

'I should imagine so.'

Hannah said, 'But what would she have to say?'

'God knows,' said Ferguson. 'But I think it's worth paying a visit, don't you?'

The Daimler left first, with Hannah and Ferguson inside, and Dillon followed in the Mini Cooper. Newton said to Cook, 'Follow them.'

'Which one?'

'We'll see where it leads.'

He phoned Marco Rossi on his mobile. 'Dillon went to Roper's house in Regency Square, then Ferguson turned up with Bernstein. They've all come out again and we're following.'

'Good, stay with it. The minute they arrive at any kind of destination, phone me.'

Brickfield Lane ran down to the Thames, a row of nine-teenth-century houses on one side, mainly renovated. The front doors opened to the street, which was the only place to park. A church was on the other side – St Mary's – and a graveyard. By the river, a path ran beside a low wall, leading to a jetty at the far end that stuck out into the water, a relic of the old days when barge traffic called in on a regular basis. There was a shop at the end of the street called Patel's, the kind that had prospered under Indian ownership, a general store.

At that time of the day, there was plenty of parking available and certainly in front of number twenty-three. The Daimler turned in and Dillon pulled up behind. Dillon was first out and went to the door. There was a bell push and beneath it a brass plate.

'George and Sara Grant,' he said, as Ferguson joined him.

Dillon pressed the bell and heard a dog barking. There was the sound of footsteps approaching, a bolt being withdrawn, the door opened on a chain. 'Be quiet, Benny,' a voice said. A face peered out, worn and lined, very grey hair pulled back from it, above faded blue eyes, and when she spoke it was almost a whisper. 'What is it?'

Hannah took over. 'Mrs Grant?'

'Yes.'

'I'm Detective Superintendent Bernstein.' She held up her warrant card. 'Special Branch, Scotland Yard. This is General Charles Ferguson.'

'We'd like a word, my dear,' Ferguson told her.

There was immediate alarm on her face. 'The police. What have I done?'

It was Dillon who interjected in excellent German. 'Don't worry, *liebling*, we're not the Gestapo. Information is what we seek.'

'But about what?'

Every instinct told him to be honest. 'About the Führer Bunker, about those last few months, and particularly about what happened to *Sturmbannführer* Max von Berger on the thirtieth of April, nineteen forty-five.'

'Oh, my God,' she said in German. 'You've come for me after all these years.' But she pulled the chain and opened the door. There was a little Scottie dog running around her ankles, yapping.

Dillon picked him up and fondled him, and the dog stopped barking and tried to lick his face. The old lady said, 'I don't understand, he never takes to strangers.'

'Oh, I have a way with dogs, ever since childhood. Benny, is it?' He handed the Scottie to her. 'All we want is a few words. There's nothing bad intended, I give you my word.'

She held the dog, looked at Dillon and touched his face with her other hand for a moment, and when she spoke it was in English. 'What's your name?'

'Dillon, ma'am.'

Her eyes became vacant for a moment. 'Yes, I believe you. You're a good man, Mr Dillon, in spite of yourself.'

Dillon almost choked and took a deep breath. 'Trust me. No harm will come to you on this earth, I swear it.'

'Then come in,' and she turned and led the way along the hall.

Newton and Cook pulled in further down Brickfield Lane, close to the shop. 'You stay here and I'll take a look,' Newton said and walked back to the house. Ferguson's chauffeur was on the other side of the road, smoking a cigarette and walking to the river. Newton quickly checked the brass plate, then returned to the car. 'Sara and George Grant. I'll have words in the shop.'

A middle-aged Indian was leaning on the counter, reading the *Evening Standard*. He glanced up, the shop for the moment quiet.

'I seem to be wasting my time as usual,' Newton said. 'Can you help me? I'm a debt collector, and I was given an Anthony Smith as being behind in payments on a car. I've come to check the address I was given. Twenty-three Brickfield Lane, only it's a Sara and George Grant.'

'You've been had,' Patel said. 'A false address. The Grants have been there for ever. Mr Grant died five years ago, Mrs Grant lives there on her own. Nice old lady, German, actually.'

'Is that so?'

'And she doesn't own a car.'

'Really. And German, you say?'

104

'Definitely. She told me her name once. Hesser – Sara Hesser. Lived there more than forty years.'

'Another wasted journey, but thanks anyway.'

Newton went back to the car, rang Marco Rossi on his mobile and explained what was going on. Rossi said, 'Stay there and I'll be in touch.'

In the sitting room at South Audley Street, the Baron was going through some papers when Marco entered. 'When you told me of your final interview with the Führer, you mentioned a secretary, an SS auxiliary called Sara Hesser.'

'Is this important?'

'It is if she's still in the land of the living and resides at twenty-three Brickfield Lane, Wapping.'

'You're certain of this?'

'Absolutely.' He told the Baron of the sequence of events. 'The fact that they've gone straight to this woman's house speaks for itself. Thank God this Indian shopkeeper knows her well or we'd have been totally in the dark. What do we do?'

'Nothing,' the Baron said. 'If the woman tells what she knows to Ferguson, he will come and see me.'

'What do you mean?'

The Baron gave him a look. 'It's time I told you something, Marco. You know of the Hitler Diary, but only what I've told you. You've never read it.'

'Yes, and I've often wondered why.'

'Because there's a secret in it. In nineteen forty-five, the Führer entered into negotiations with President Roosevelt in an effort to promote a negotiated peace. The idea was for the Germans and Americans to turn on the Russians, to defeat a common enemy. Roosevelt didn't buy it – but he did discuss it. Hitler sent General Walter Schellenberg of the SS to Sweden – and Roosevelt sent an American multi-millionaire and senator named Jake Cazalet.'

There was a moment's silence, then Marco said, 'But that's the name of the President of the United States.'

'And of Jake Cazalet's father. He was a member of Roosevelt's kitchen cabinet. Has it occurred to you how that would look? That Roosevelt, with Cazalet as his agent, actually had such dealings with Hitler? True, it didn't come to anything, but what capital America's enemies around the world would make of it! Cazalet would be finished.' He smiled. 'I've held this secret for years, always certain it would eventually be of great importance.'

'It's unbelievable.'

'So we wait for Ferguson.' The Baron smiled again. 'But that doesn't mean we can't have a drink on it.'

The sitting room was crowded, not only with furniture, but with the bric-a-brac accumulated over a long life. An old grand piano stood in a corner, the top crowded with photos, some in silver frames, the largest of a handsome young man in the uniform of an army captain.

Ferguson picked it up. 'Your husband?'

'Yes, that's George. He was a military policeman. I was an interpreter. That's how we met.' She sat down, clutching Benny on her lap. 'I was interrogated, you know, by the intelligence people, about being on the staff in the Bunker.'

Ferguson nodded to Hannah, who said, 'Tell us about that, Mrs Grant.'

'There's nothing really to tell. I was an SS auxiliary, a secretary, a typist. I was twenty-two years old. I was transferred from SD headquarters in Berlin. SD meant SS Intelligence, but I was, like I've told you, just a young office girl.'

'So you were there for six months? Until April forty-five and the final catastrophe?' Hannah asked.

'That's right. I was a relief secretary, the most junior of all. I made the coffee, that sort of thing.'

Dillon was filled with an enormous compassion for this woman, already old and, more than that, old beyond her years, a woman who had been at the sharp edge of history, but also a woman who was lying.

'So you knew the Führer?' Hannah asked.

'Of course, but the others were far more important than me, the other secretaries, I mean.'

Hannah nodded. 'And *Sturmbannführer* Baron von Berger? You knew him?'

'Oh, yes.' The old lady stroked Benny's head. 'He was in the Bunker for the last three months. Wounded in Russia. He came to be decorated and the Führer took a fancy to him, made him an aide.'

'I see. Was there anything special about him?'

'No,' the old lady said. 'The last couple of days were terrible, everything was confused. Then the Führer and his wife committed suicide and we all scattered, ran for it. A lot of us went through the underground tunnels. Some of us made it. I reached the West and the Americans a couple of weeks later.' She shook her head, as if looking back into a past that she didn't want to see. 'But I went through all this with the British intelligence people all those years ago.'

Ferguson interrupted, 'So you didn't see anything of von Berger at the end?'

She shrugged. 'He was there and then he wasn't, but that was true of so many people.'

Hannah carried on. 'And yet we know that von Berger escaped from Berlin in a Storch aircraft. He was a prisoner of war for a couple of years, then became a hugely successful businessman.'

'I know nothing of that. Please believe me. I was just a relief secretary, nobody of any importance.' She said almost vacantly, 'I made the coffee,' and because she was old and tired and her guard was down, she added, 'The Führer liked

107

it black and not too strong. The second cup he liked with brown sugar. Of course at the end, he had the palsy. His hands shook very much and I had to pour for him. He had to lift the cup with both hands. It was very awkward when he was dictating.'

In the astonished silence which followed, Hannah said, 'The Führer dictated to you? But you told us you were a nobody!'

The old woman looked at her, dazed, put a hand to her face, and Dillon, in one of the cruellest acts of his life, shouted at her in German, '*Fräulein* Hesser, you have been less than honest. You will speak.'

Hannah started to protest, 'For God's sake, Sean –'

But he pushed her aside and towered over the old lady. 'You took dictation from the Führer, didn't you?'

'Yes.' She was terrified.

'What kind of dictation? Explain.'

Her head shook from side to side frantically. 'No, I dare not, I swore a holy oath to serve the Führer.'

Already hating himself, Dillon raised his voice and thundered at her, 'What was so special? You *will* tell me.'

She broke then and answered him in German. 'Each day for six months, he dictated his diary to me.'

Hannah spoke excellent German, and Ferguson spoke enough to understand. 'Dear God in heaven, Hitler's bloody diary,' he said.

Dillon knelt down and kissed Sara Hesser on the forehead. 'I'm sorry I frightened you. It's all right now.' He hugged her. 'Just one more thing. What you said about Max von Berger. It wasn't true, was it?'

Her eyes had filled with tears. 'No. He was there in the Führer's study on the thirtieth. I was there, too. The Führer had a mission for him. To fly out of Berlin in a plane hidden in Goebbels' garage.'

'To do what?' Hannah asked.

'Why, to save the diary. A holy book, the Führer called it. He said it must never be copied.'

Ferguson said, 'The diary was completely up to date then?'

'Oh, yes, up to that very day. I covered the last six months of the war. All the traitors, all those who let him down, accounts of everything. His attempts to negotiate a peace with President Roosevelt. The secret meetings in Sweden.'

The silence was breathtaking. 'His what?' Charles Ferguson whispered.

'Oh, yes,' she said. 'I wrote down every word, General, and in spite of the years, I remember everything.' Which was exactly what she proceeded to tell them.

They left half an hour later and paused by the Daimler. 'God, you were a bastard back there,' Hannah said to Dillon.

'He certainly was,' Ferguson said. 'But it worked.'

'It was all those years ago, but the SS training never goes away,' Dillon said. 'The shouted command, the harsh voice, and the response is a reflex.'

'Anyway, now we know where Max von Berger's millions came from,' Ferguson said.

'And can't do a thing about it,' Hannah said.

'We're also in possession of the uncomfortable fact that in nineteen forty-five, Hitler made a peace overture to Roosevelt, and Roosevelt took it seriously enough to send Jake Cazalet's father to Sweden to discuss it with Hitler's representative,' Ferguson said.

'But, sir, if nothing came of it, does it matter?' Hannah said.

'Oh yes, my dear, it most certainly does. And the involvement of the President's father makes it worse. The media would have a field day. Roosevelt, Cazalet and Hitler.' He shook his head. 'It could do the President great harm.'

'And at the worst, finish him,' Dillon said.

'Yes. Come on. Let's go see von Berger.'

'I'm your man,' said Dillon, and hurried to his car.

As the Daimler drove away, Hannah said to Ferguson, 'I hope the old lady will be all right, sir.'

'Yes, I'm sorry about that, but it had to be done.'

'What do you intend to say to the Baron?'

Ferguson smiled. 'I haven't the slightest idea, Superintendent.'

Newton and Cook let them leave and then followed. Twenty minutes later, Newton called. 'We're just passing the Dorchester. They're turning into South Audley Street.'

'Fine. Hang around, in case I need you.'

Rossi switched off his phone and turned. 'It would seem they intend to pay us a visit.'

Max von Berger smiled. 'Well, that should be interesting.'

At the Rashid house, a maid in a black dress and white apron opened the door. Hannah said, 'Is Baron von Berger at home? General Ferguson would like a word.'

'Yes, miss, but you're expected. Please follow me.'

She led the way upstairs from the hall and opened the door to the drawing room, where the Baron sat by the fire, Marco standing by the window.

'General, what a surprise. What can I do for you?'

Ferguson turned to Hannah. 'Tell him, Superintendent.'

Afterwards, the Baron shook his head. 'An amazing story. Ridiculous, of course, but then what would one expect from an old lady who obviously went through traumatic times in the war. She obviously suffers from some delusion, some fantasy that she knew the Führer. I was an aide in the Bunker for three months and certainly knew the staff. I can't recall a Sara Hesser.'

'Well, you would say that, ould son, wouldn't you?' Dillon told him.

'Mind you, I'm intrigued by the whole idea,' the Baron said. 'Perhaps the Superintendent could give me the view from Scotland Yard. If, for example, I *were* in control of deposits in private accounts in Switzerland, would that constitute a crime in the UK?'

Hannah glanced at Ferguson. 'No, sir, it would not.'

'And if someone gave you their diary for safekeeping, would that be illegal?'

'Of course not, but –'

'For God's sake, let's cut the nonsense and get down to facts,' Ferguson said. 'We now know the truth about how you got out of Berlin and why. We also know the source of your money – the money that got you started again after the war. And then there's the diary: a holy book, Sara Hesser said.'

'A most fanciful idea.'

'Especially when it records meetings in Sweden between Hitler's go-between and President Cazalet's father.'

'As I said, a fanciful idea.' The Baron smiled. 'Though it certainly wouldn't help Jake Cazalet's political future much, would it?' He smiled again. 'But all this is nonsense. Stories of the Führer's diary have abounded for years. Charlatans and forgers have tried to produce such items repeatedly. Now, we have the fantasy of some old lady. No, it won't do.'

'Even if both British and German records indicate that she was indeed there in the Bunker?'

'Oh, really? Hmm. Well, there you are then. I'm afraid there's no more I can add, General – though if all of this *were* true, the prospect of it being revealed would be very unpleasant for the President, I should think. You take my meaning?'

'I certainly do.' Ferguson nodded to Hannah and Dillon. 'Let's go,' and he led the way out.

Marco poured an Irish whiskey and took it to his father. 'Bravo, you deserve it. He never knew what hit him.'

'Ferguson is a very astute man, Marco. He won't let it go – and this thing could easily leak.'

'But wouldn't that accomplish your aim? To hurt the President?'

'But I don't want it to happen *yet*. I want it to be on my terms and at a time to suit me.' He sipped his whiskey. 'But the game is in motion now. The ball, as the English say, is in Ferguson's court.' He sighed. 'Hitler offered her a seat in my plane. It would have got her out and she refused, said it was her duty to stay with him.' He shook his head. 'She should have died with the others.'

Marco lit a cigarette and walked to the window, staring out into South Audley Street. 'Yes, it really would have been better when you think of it.'

7

March weather, dusk falling early, rain drifting in across the Thames, and in the darkness of the porch of the church in Brickfield Lane, Marco Rossi waited in a black trench coat and rain hat.

Rossi wasn't sure what he intended to do, and had certainly not mentioned to the Baron what he was up to, and yet, there was a certain inevitability to things. He hadn't driven in his own car and had taken a taxi to Wapping High Street and walked the rest of the way, which perhaps meant something.

He'd been there an hour, watching the house, not sure what he was waiting for, and then a light went on over the door, it creaked open and the old lady appeared with the Scottie on a lead. She was wearing a head scarf and a raincoat and put up an umbrella.

'Good boy, Benny,' she said, and set off down the pavement for the corner shop, whose lights were still on.

Rossi hurried along the other side of the churchyard and paused at the end by the wall opposite the shop where the old jetty jutted out into the river. There was no rail, just a single lamp giving a subdued glow. The old lady turned onto the jetty and walked to the end with Benny. Rossi, seizing his opportunity, darted up behind her as she gazed out at the bright lights of a riverboat passing by, put both hands on her back and pushed her over into the water.

She had released her grip on the lead and the dog barked and ran to the edge of the jetty. Rossi looked down, saw her flounder and go under. He dashed away as quickly as he had come to the shelter of the churchyard, and from there made his way back to Wapping High Street.

It was perhaps twenty minutes later that Mr Patel, distracted by Benny's constant barking, went outside and found the little dog, still with his lead on him, at the end of the jetty.

'What is it, Benny?' Patel demanded as he retrieved his lead. Then he looked over and saw her frail body half in the water below.

The following morning, Charles Ferguson was having breakfast when his phone rang.

'Sir, it's Bernstein.'

'Isn't this a bit early, even for you, Superintendent?'

'Just listen, sir. I put Mrs Sara Grant on the Special Branch Priority One list, just to keep an eye on her.'

'And?'

'She was found in the Thames last night, just off that jetty at the end of Brickfield Lane. The Indian gentleman, Mr Patel, who owns the store, heard the dog barking and went to investigate. He found it at the end of the jetty with its lead still on and she was in the water.'

'Dear God,' Ferguson said. 'Where is she now?'

'Wapping Mortuary.'

'Oh, we're such idiots, Superintendent. Look, we'll have to fast-track the post-mortem. I'll telephone Professor George Langley, and ask him to do it this morning.'

'That *is* fast, sir.'

'He'll do it for me. You will use your authority to take over the case from the Wapping police. It's a Code One matter from now on. I'll sign the warrant. Brook no interference from anyone. And notify Dillon.'

Dillon was on his morning run from Stable Mews, the hood of his tracksuit up against a light drizzle, when his mobile sounded and Hannah said, 'It's me, Sean.'

'At this time in the morning. Jesus, girl, am I finally getting through to you?'

'Shut up, Sean, it's bad news,' and she told him. Dillon stopped in a doorway, stunned. 'Are you still there, Sean?'

'Yes, I'm here.'

'What do you think?'

'It stinks, that's what I think.'

The rage was in his voice. She said, 'Sean, don't do anything stupid. We have to be sure. George Langley will do the postmortem later this morning. He's the best there is. He's put more murderers behind bars than even you can imagine. If there's the smallest thing wrong, he'll find it.'

'He'd better,' Dillon said. 'By God, he'd better.'

She rang off and Dillon stayed there for a while in the doorway, then walked away.

He went home and changed, then drove to Roper's place and found him in the sitting room at the computers. The Major said, 'You're early. That means something's up.'

Dillon told him, then went and found the bottle of Paddy whiskey and poured a glass. 'It's early, even for me, but I need it.' He swallowed it down. 'What do you think?'

'She was certainly a mine of information.'

'Which von Berger immediately denied as the fantasy of an old woman.'

'Who promptly has some sort of accident and ends up in the Thames. Very useful, that happening,' Roper said.

'Yes. It's all true, everything she told us. Von Berger's mission from Hitler, his final flight out of Berlin, the diary – all true.'

'And now the source of that information is dead,' Roper said.

Dillon's face was drawn. 'I told her to trust me. I swore no harm would come to her. You know what she said to me? "You're a good man, Mr Dillon, in spite of yourself."'

'I'm sorry, Sean.'

'I know somebody who'll be a damn sight sorrier when I've finished with them.'

'Wait for the post-mortem.'

'Of course I will.' Dillon looked like the Devil himself as he left.

It was the middle of the afternoon when Ferguson, Hannah and Dillon arrived at Wapping Mortuary, in response to Professor Langley's call. The reception area was pleasant enough, and Hannah went to the desk and spoke to a young woman, who picked up a phone.

'I'm sorry, Professor Langley is just cleaning up. He'll be with you shortly.'

Ferguson and Hannah sat down, Dillon lit a cigarette and stood looking out of the window. Ferguson said, 'You seem restless, Dillon.'

'No, angry.'

'Calm yourself, we'll have the result soon.'

'We have that now. The only result was her death and don't tell me it could have been a coincidence. Neither you nor I believe in them very much, not in our business.'

Before Ferguson could reply, a small grey-haired, energetic man entered. 'Hello, Charles.'

Ferguson shook hands. 'Thanks for rushing this through, George. Detective Superintendent Bernstein here is the case officer. Sean Dillon is a colleague.'

'Sorry about the delay. Would you care to see the body?'

It was Dillon who cut in. 'Yes, very much.'

Ferguson nodded and Langley said, 'This way then.'

The room he led them to was lined with white tiles. The fluorescent lighting was strangely harsh, and several steel operating tables stood in a line. There was a body on the first one, covered with a white sheet.

'Mrs Sara Grant. Do you know this woman personally, Charles?'

'We all do.'

'I'll just show you her face then. The rest is rather unpleasant. Autopsies usually are.'

She looked surprisingly calm, even the lines on her face seemingly smoothed, at peace in a way.

'Not a mark on her,' Ferguson said.

'Nor anywhere,' Langley said. 'There was no fight here, no blows or wounds. The only reason for death was drowning.'

Dillon said, 'You're certain of that?'

'Absolutely. I noticed in the police report that the local shopkeeper who found her regularly saw her at night walking her dog along the jetty. She liked to stand at the end and watch the boats. I've visited the spot myself. There's no handrail and a thirty-foot drop into the river.'

'You're sure there were no marks at all, Professor?' Hannah said. 'No indication of any kind of a struggle?'

'Not even bruising from the fall into the water. Of course, she was wearing a trouser suit and a heavy overcoat.'

'Is there anything else you can tell us?'

'Only that she had lung cancer. Wouldn't have lasted more than a few months, anyway. Death by drowning, Charles, that's the best I can do.'

'Dammit,' Dillon said. 'There has to be more.'

'No, Mr Dillon, she fell from the end of the jetty and drowned. Now, as to whether she had any help – which I know is what

117

you're wondering about – I couldn't possibly comment on that. All I can say is that there are no signs of bruising, which on a woman as old and frail as she was means no violence of even the mildest kind.' He turned to Ferguson. 'Charles, I realize that this is probably some sort of intelligence matter and no doubt classified. I'm happy not to know any more.'

'Many thanks, George.' Ferguson shook hands.

Dillon said, 'That's it then, nothing?'

'Sorry, Mr Dillon.' Langley walked to the door with them. 'Oh, wait a minute, there was something else.'

'And what would that be?' Ferguson demanded.

'I've done thousands of post-mortems over the years and this was a first for me. The number tattooed in her left armpit. Not on the arm, like in the concentration camps, but in the armpit. It means she served in the SS.' He smiled. 'But then you would know more about that than me, Charles.'

In the back of the Daimler, Dillon pulled the glass screen across, cutting off the chauffeur.

'They did it, General, the bastards took her out.'

'But how?' Hannah said. 'We never mentioned any address.'

'Oh, come on, Hannah. Once they knew she existed, how long do you think it took Rossi to trace her?'

'But –'

'That's enough,' said Ferguson. 'Squabbling won't bring her back. Superintendent, get von Berger on the line for me.'

It was Marco who answered the phone and passed it to his father. 'General,' the Baron said. 'What now?'

'*Fräulein* Sara Hesser has turned up in the Thames. It's time for us to talk – now.'

'Why?'

'Would you prefer me to present a warrant and make it official?'

'There's no need for the crudities, General. I'll tell you what – let's make it civilized. The Piano Bar at the Dorchester. Let's say seven?'

'All right. And bring your thug with you.'

He hung up.

The Baron handed the phone back to Rossi. 'He doesn't seem to like you much. Marco – Sara Hesser was discovered in the Thames today.'

'My God.' Rossi managed to sound horrified.

'Do you know anything about this?'

'Father, on my life, I swear to you . . .'

The Baron raised a hand. 'Well, Ferguson obviously thinks we do. It should be an interesting evening. And just to make sure, remember this: Newton and Cook don't exist and we've never heard of Brickfield Lane.'

Only half a dozen people were in the Piano Bar when Ferguson arrived with Dillon and Hannah. Dillon wandered over to the piano, as he often did, and began to play: 'A Foggy Day in London Town'. Hannah came and leaned on the piano. 'I've never understood this, Sean, the piano. You seem to be good at so many things.'

'You mean like killing people?' He smiled. 'Don't be deceived, Hannah, good barroom piano is all.'

'You're angry. That always worries me.'

'Yes, good and angry. I'm a bad man, Hannah. I've walked over plenty of corpses, but there's something about Sara Hesser's death that grinds at me. She deserved better.'

The waiter was pouring champagne when Max von Berger and Rossi appeared at the top of the steps by the bar.

The Baron sat opposite Ferguson and Hannah. Rossi and Dillon stood, in a way confronting each other.

'So what is this about, General?'

'Tell him, Superintendent.'

When she was finished, the Baron sighed. 'So this poor lady falls off the jetty and your Professor Langley confirms she died of drowning, with no suspicious circumstances. So what does this have to do with me?'

'The fact that she died at all is a suspicious circumstance,' Dillon said.

Marco Rossi said, 'You don't have a leg to stand on, Dillon. This meeting is not only futile, it's offensive.'

'Enough,' Ferguson said. 'We're not talking legalities, we're talking truth. We may not be able to arrest you, but you know and we know what happened.'

'I know no such thing,' said the Baron. 'Really, Marco is right. This is most offensive.' The Baron stood.

Dillon said to Rossi, 'What did you do, push her over?'

Rossi took a step towards him and Hannah grabbed Sean's arm. 'Let it go.'

The Baron's face was grim. 'I think we'll leave now,' and he walked out, followed by his son.

In the car outside, he said quietly, 'You had nothing to do with this? Swear it to me.'

'On my life. She was an old woman who had a tragic accident. That's all.'

'But, as Ferguson puts it, most fortunate for us.'

That his son was lying naturally occurred to him, but he pushed the thought away and leaned back.

In his own car, Ferguson clicked off his phone, and immediately dialled again, his direct Codex Four line to the Basement office at the White House. Johnson, at his desk, answered at once.

'Yes?'

'Ferguson.'

'Charles, how goes it?'

'Rather badly. I've just talked to the Prime Minister. He wants me to go to Washington immediately and speak to the President personally. I'll bring Dillon with me.'

'Sorry, Charles, but the President's gone to his house on Nantucket for the weekend. Can I do anything?'

'It's a very grave matter that affects him personally.'

There was a pause. 'All right, go straight to Andrews Air Force Base. They'll take you there by helicopter and make a beach landing. I'll arrange it.' He hesitated. 'This is a bad one, Charles?'

'Very much so.'

'Then I'll get down there myself.'

'I think that would be wise, old boy. You'll be going to war again, I assure you.' He hung up.

Johnson sat there at his desk, frowning, then picked up the phone and rang the President on his direct line.

NANTUCKET

8

The Daimler arrived at Farley Field, was passed through by RAF police, and drove to where the Citation Ten waited, the Airstair door down.

Squadron Leader Lacey and Flight Lieutenant Parry stood waiting. Both held the Air Force Cross, an acknowledgement of many hazardous missions on Ferguson's behalf; on more than one occasion, they'd dropped Sean Dillon by parachute into uncertain landings. They were essential parts of Ferguson's tightly knit, highly secret group. Both were in RAF uniform.

'I see you've dressed appropriately for once,' Ferguson said.

'Some of our closest friends are at Andrews Air Force Base, sir.'

'You're right.'

An RAF sergeant, a small energetic woman, came down the steps. 'June Walters, General. I'll be looking after you. Follow me, please.'

She led the way as Ferguson obeyed.

'Hello, boys,' Dillon said. 'Here we go again.'

Lacey said, 'Is this serious business, Sean?'

'Well, I wouldn't book any out-of-season holidays for the next few weeks.'

'Terrific,' Parry said. 'It's always so interesting when you appear.'

'Nice plane,' Dillon said.

'Yes. Brand new. Do you like it? Fastest commercial plane in the world next to the Concorde,' Lacey told him.

'That's impressive. Let's get on with it, then,' and Dillon went up into the aircraft.

They took off shortly afterwards, fast-tracked by air traffic control as a priority-one flight, climbed steadily west, and had lifted to fifty thousand feet as they reached the Atlantic. Sergeant Walters appeared.

'I've got minestrone soup, melon, steak, new potatoes and vegetables.' She turned to Dillon. 'I understand you like plain food, sir. There's an item called an Irish potato pie – lamb, onion and dumplings.'

Dillon said, 'Jesus, woman, that's what you call plain food?'

She smiled. 'Apparently. A drink, gentlemen?'

'Bring me a Bushmills whiskey and open a bottle of a halfway decent champagne and we'll share it.' She restrained laughter, glanced at Ferguson, who nodded, and she went away.

Dillon lit a cigarette. 'So, what are you going to say to Cazalet?'

'The truth about this whole affair as we know it.'

'And what will he say?'

'God knows. He's an admirable and decent man, and he's suffered many blows in his personal life. His wife died of leukaemia; his father, the elder Jake Cazalet who figures so prominently in the diary, was killed in a car accident years ago. The kidnapping of his daughter, no one knows better than you. It was you and Blake who saved her.'

Dillon held out his hand, took the whiskey Sergeant Walters offered, and swallowed it. 'But if this von Berger thing leaks, the great American public won't give a stuff about what's gone before, will it?'

Sergeant Walters handed them a glass of champagne each.
'You're a cynic, Sean,' Ferguson said.
'A realist, but there you go, calling me by my first name again.'
'Which means?'
'That you want me to handle it the hard way.' He raised
his glass. 'Cheers, Charlie.'
'Cheers, Sean. You're always so dependable.'

On the beach at the old family house at Nantucket, the
President walked with his favourite Secret Service man, an
enormous black ex-Marine named Clancy Smith, and Blake
Johnson. The President's dog, Murchison, a flat-coat retriever,
ran in and out of the surf. The sea was rough, the wind
keen. Cazalet spoke to Clancy and asked for a cigarette, and
Clancy lit a Marlboro inside his coat and passed it.

Blake said, 'I've told you before, sir, there are voters who
would hold that against you.'

'We're all entitled to a weakness, Blake, and these things
got you and me through the Vietnam War.' Murchison jumped
up and he patted him. 'Now if I should beat this wonderful
dog, *that* would lose me votes by the thousands.'

Blake lit a cigarette for himself inside his storm coat. 'I
give in, Mr President.'

'So, Ferguson gave you no idea of what all this is about?'
'Only that it's a bad one.'

'Then that's bad enough.' There was a roaring in the
distance, and they turned and saw the helicopter landing on
the beach beside the house.

'God, the sound of those things. It always takes me back
to the war,' Cazalet said. 'Let's go and greet our guests and
see what's gone wrong.'

Cazalet had always cherished his quiet weekends at Nantucket.
He preferred to have only the housekeeper-cum-cook, Mrs

Boulder, organize things, and bring in whoever she needed to clean or run the place when he wasn't there. So when they sat down in the large drawing room, it was only Cazalet, Blake and Smith, with Ferguson and Dillon sitting opposite. Ferguson covered the entire story. There was silence.

The President said, 'Obviously, Blake informed me of the events at Kate Rashid's funeral, but this – I never expected anything like this.'

There was another pause. Blake said, 'Is it really that bad, Mr President? It's not as if anything actually happened.'

Dillon said, 'May I speak, sir?'

'Of course.'

'Your father, Senator Jake Cazalet – his position in all this is clear. He acted, under orders and in good faith, as President Roosevelt's man in a most delicate and secret situation.'

'That is true.'

'In a strange way, Hitler's emissary, General Walter Schellenberg of the SS, was in a similar situation. He was not a Nazi Party member. In fact, after the war he was tried and found guilty only of being a member of an illegal organization, the SS.'

'So?'

'I could be found guilty of being a member of the IRA for more years than I care to remember, but that wouldn't change what Schellenberg personally felt. He was simply the Führer's mouthpiece and your father was Roosevelt's mouthpiece.'

'Dillon, watch yourself,' Ferguson said.

'No.' Cazalet put his hand up. 'He's right.'

Dillon nodded. 'But you need to explore deeper than that, because, as sure as hell, the press will.'

'What do you mean?' Blake asked.

'Well, many experts would say that Roosevelt perhaps *did* show an interest, because Hitler's overtures included the idea

128

of halting the Red Menace seeping into Western Europe. So let's say Roosevelt toyed with the idea, or why bother sending Cazalet in the first place?'

It was Cazalet who said, 'Go on.'

'But he considers all the facts and changes his mind. That change of mind would be what all the experts, and the press, would seize on.'

'What the hell are you talking about, Dillon?' Ferguson asked.

'That close to the end of things, the American army crossed the Elbe. General George Patton's tanks could have roared up the autobahn and reached Berlin in twenty-four hours. Only they didn't. They were ordered to stay where they were by Eisenhower, because Roosevelt had decided, after word from Stalin, that the Russians were entitled to seize Berlin. And so began forty-five years of Cold War. Not to mention one hundred thousand German women raped.'

There was a heavy silence, and it was Jake Cazalet who said, 'You're right. Everything you say is right.'

'Everything I say is what the world will seize on. Because the President sent him there, your father will be part of it, and because he was your father, you, sir, will be part of it. In my opinion, that is what Baron Max von Berger has already worked out.'

Everyone stirred uneasily. It was Blake who said, 'Then how on earth can one combat him? Do we try pre-empting the whole thing? Spilling the story first?'

It was Ferguson who said, 'It's the story that's the trouble.'

'I agree,' the President said. 'And the trouble is, gentlemen, I'm engaged in world affairs of great moment. To be arguing with the United Nations over Iraq, with the threat of a scandal like this hanging over us – it would be a disaster. My opponents at home would rip me to pieces. Our enemies abroad would immediately take advantage.'

'So that means –?' Ferguson said, looking directly at the President.

Cazalet smiled, but there was no humour to it.

'Mr Dillon?' he said. 'If we had that diary . . .'

Dillon nodded. 'I'll see what we can do, sir.' He looked at Johnson. 'You up for it, Blake?'

Blake grinned. 'I'm your man, Sean.'

LONDON
SCOTLAND
IRELAND

9

Meanwhile, Marco Rossi, trawling the security files at Rashid Investments, had discovered the scale of Kate Rashid's involvement, not only in southern Arabia, but nearer to home in Ireland. In fact, she'd had very active arms deals brewing with both dissident IRA and Protestant Loyalist groups. Kate had been very even-handed.

There was one name in particular he knew, a man once big with the Ulster Defence Association, who, after a very public row, had moved to the Red Hand of Ulster, probably the most extremist Loyalist organization of all.

The sums of money involved were quite staggering. No sense letting that all go to waste, he thought.

This explained why he was walking through Kilburn, the most Irish area of London, on a dark evening, in a black bomber jacket, a Walther PPK snug against his back, to meet one Patrick Murphy. Mr Murphy was the landlord of a public house called the Orange George, its outside wall painted in a way reminiscent of a Protestant area in Belfast.

Marco listened to the Irish music, then went in. The pub was full, and an Irish band was playing. He stood at one end, and a good-looking, middle-aged woman came up.

'Patrick Murphy is expecting me.'

'Is that so.' She looked him over and smiled. 'You're not having me on?'

He reached over and stroked her cheek. 'I'd love to, and maybe later, but Pat Murphy is expecting me. Just say Marco. What's your name?'

'Janet.'

'Well, who knows, Janet?'

She flushed and went into the back, more excited than she had been in a long time.

Murphy was sitting in the back room, a late-middle-aged man with a belly on him, an account book open on the table, when Janet showed Marco in.

'Ah, Mr Rossi. You'd better sit down.' He nodded to Janet, who went out. He reached for a whiskey bottle and a couple of glasses and poured.

'Good health.' He drank his whiskey. Marco ignored his and lit a cigarette.

'So, where are we?'

Murphy said, 'I was quite thrown to get your phone call. I mean, Derry Gibson. How would I be knowing a desperate character like that?'

Marco saw him for what he was, a small man, a go-between, useful in his way, probably in love with the idea that he was some kind of rebel.

'You'd know him because you had dealings with Kate Rashid a year ago, and brokered a meeting for her with Derry Gibson, who had money from the drug trade and wanted to buy arms. Two cargoes off-loaded in County Down earlier this year, and a third was arranged just before Kate Rashid's unfortunate death. A two-million-pound deal was supposed to take place in a week.'

'I don't know Derry Gibson.'

'Then I'm wasting my time here. I'll have to find another buyer for those AK47s and Stinger missiles. Maybe the IRA.' Marco picked up the glass, swallowed the whiskey and stood up.

The rear door creaked open and a hard, tough-looking man of around forty-five walked in, with blond hair, wearing a jacket in Donegal tweed, and an open-necked black shirt. His voice had the distinctive Ulster accent. In a strange way, it reminded Marco of Dillon's.

'Just hold it right there. I'm Derry Gibson.'

'Why, what a surprise,' Marco said. 'And me thinking you were at Drumgoole on the Down Coast.'

'Well, I was, until this idiot phoned me yesterday, so you might say I've flown here in a hurry. What's going on?'

'It's simple. You used to deal with Kate Rashid. Now she's dead, and my father, Baron Max von Berger, has taken over the firm. I'm Marco Rossi, as I'm sure you know, and I'm in charge of all security matters for Rashid and Berger.'

'Is that so?'

'Yes and some other affairs, as well. Though, to be frank, with all her money, I wonder why Kate bothered with little deals like this. Two million? She was a romantic, I suppose.'

And the strange thing was, Gibson's face changed. 'Damn you, don't you put her down. She was a great lady.'

One hand went inside his jacket and Marco said, 'Tell you what. Let's both put our cards on the table. And everything else.' He reached behind him, found the Walther and set it down in front of him.

Derry Gibson hesitated, then took a Walther of his own from his right pocket and laid it on the table, as well. 'You've got good taste in guns. Let's talk.'

'I've got a Spanish deep-sea trawler, the *Mona Lisa*, that should do the trick,' Rossi said. 'Italian registration. European fishery regulations allow it to be there. It can drop off at Drumgoole on the night indicated. No problem.' Marco smiled. 'I'm not going to say hold out the cash as soon as we beach, because I know you know how to play the game. You'll want to make more deals.'

'And you, Mr Rossi. I wonder why you're doing this. You've got money, too, I understand.'

'Yes, but it keeps things interesting. I like the action, Gibson, always did. In fact, when the *Mona Lisa* turns up in Drumgoole, I'll be on board. I'll go out from the Isle of Man by another boat and join her.'

'All right. We'll have a whiskey on it.' Gibson picked up the bottle.

Marco said, 'No, there's more. I require a favour, here in London. Would you happen to know a gangster called Harry Salter, and his nephew, Billy?'

It was Murphy, standing by the back door, who exploded. 'Real villains, those two. Harry Salter was one of the top guvnors in the East End, big as the Krays. He's gone legit in the last few years, supposedly. Mind you, the whisper is that he's into cigarette smuggling in a big way, from Holland. The profit is enormous.'

'It pays better than heroin,' Gibson said.

'You would know.'

'I might. What have you got against Salter?'

Marco said, 'Have you ever heard of a fellow countryman of yours, once a big man with the IRA, called Sean Dillon?'

Gibson said, 'Everyone in our business knows Dillon, that bloody Fenian bastard. Works for the Brits now.'

'You know about that?'

'Of course. Charles-bloody-Ferguson. He's been the scourge of the IRA for years, but he doesn't do the Loyalist side any favours, ould Charles, and with Sean as his good right hand, he's a difficult man to deal with.'

136

'You sound like you know Dillon personally.'

'We've exchanged shots. We were once in the same sewer in Derry after a riot – the British Army always had difficulty in telling the difference between the IRA and the Prods. It was Dillon who got me out to the river. He said "Keep running. Only don't run back to me, or I'll kill you."' He poured another whiskey. 'He kills everyone, that's what they say about him.' He stared into his glass. 'But he got me out of the sewer and I was the enemy. I've always wondered why he did that.'

'Don't ask me, I'm not into philosophy. The thing is, Charles Ferguson and the Rashid family had a huge feud. You may have heard of how the three brothers came to a bad end? Dillon killed all of them.'

'And Kate Rashid?'

'Oh, he had something to do with that, too, and so did Ferguson and the Salters. Let's put it this way. I'd like to cause them a lot of grief.'

'You mean of the permanent variety?'

'Not yet. First, a bit of mischief. I hear that Salter runs riverboats, amongst other things.'

'That's right, up and down the Thames,' Murphy said. 'Westminster, Charing Cross piers, better than the bus.'

'Including a boat called the *River Queen*?'

'That's his pride and joy. Originally built in the thirties. He's spent a fortune refurbishing her,' Murphy said. 'Lovely boat.'

'Excellent.' Marco turned to Gibson. 'Sink her for me. Do that, and the deal arranged with Kate Rashid for your arms shipment goes through. Delivery at Drumgoole on the tenth.'

Derry looked astonished. 'That's only four days away.'

'The *Mona Lisa's* already left Spain. I assumed you'd be a sensible man.'

Gibson laughed. 'Oh, it's a pleasure doing business with you, Mr Rossi. As for this business with the Salters, that'll be a pleasure, too.'

It was past midnight when Gibson and Murphy drove down to Wapping in a Land Rover, past the Dark Man and along Cable Wharf, where the *River Queen* was berthed. It was an area still undeveloped, mainly decaying warehouses. It was dark, a few lights on the other side, but no traffic on the river because of the hour. No one was around, or so it seemed.

Unfortunately, life being as uncertain as usual, there was a movement from one of a stack of packing cases, where an old drunk, a tramp named Wally Brown, habitually kipped with his few wretched possessions. Disturbed by the noise, he crept out and listened.

'Jesus, Derry, I don't like it.'

'Murphy, it's as simple as hell. I go down through the engine-room hatch and open the seacocks. Water pours in and the boat sinks. Now, do as you're told and we'll be out of here before you know it. Fuck me up and you'll end up in the river, too.'

'There's no need for that, Derry.'

'Yes, well, this arms deal with Rossi means a lot to me. With that final arms shipment, I'll be ready to take on the IRA for real. It'll be just like the old days, the great days.'

'I'm your man, Derry, I won't let you down.'

'Then let's get on with it.'

They went up the gangplank to the *River Queen*, and Wally Brown, having heard everything, crept back and cowered inside his packing case.

Murphy stayed on deck to stand guard, Gibson slid back the engine-room hatch, only switching on his light when he'd descended the steel ladder. The engines were beautiful,

138

everything was beautiful and as an Irish boy raised in a fishing port, he felt genuine regret.

'What a beauty,' he said softly. 'Still . . .'

He knew there would be at least four seacocks and checked them out, sturdy circular wheels in bronze. The first one turned very smoothly, then clicked to a halt. He hurriedly moved to the second. By the time he was working on the fourth, water was already sloshing along the floor of the engine room and he was ankle-deep.

He came out and joined Murphy. 'You cast off forward and I'll see to the stern line, quick now, then get ashore.'

They did that, then pulled up the gangplank and stood back from the edge of the wharf and watched the *River Queen* drift out a little and settle.

'A sad sight,' Gibson said, as water poured across the deck. 'But we've done our worst. It's the early-morning flight to Belfast for me. If I need you, I'll be in touch.'

'I know one thing,' Murphy said, as he got into the Land Rover. 'Harry Salter won't be pleased.'

He wasn't. Dillon, on his morning run, answered his mobile and heard Harry say, 'Some damn bastard's sunk the *River Queen* at her moorings.'

'What do you mean?' Dillon asked.

'Well, the bleeding boat didn't just sink on her own! Billy's got his scuba-diving gear out. He's going down to take a look.'

'Ah, Harry, he shouldn't be doing that, not after having been shot to hell in Hazar only a few months ago. I'll come straight down.'

He switched off, thought about it and then rang Ferguson at Cavendish Place.

At the end of Cable Wharf, he found Harry, Joe Baxter and Sam Hall looking across at the part of the *River Queen* that was sticking out of the water. Billy's Shogun was parked nearby, the rear door open to reveal various items of diving equipment and a couple of air bottles.

'Where's Billy?' Dillon said, as he got out of the Mini.

'He's been in the water for fifteen minutes.'

'Dammit, Harry, he shouldn't have gone down there. Leave it to the salvage experts.'

Then two things happened. Ferguson and Hannah arrived, and Billy surfaced. He slipped off his air bottle and Dillon reached for it. Billy started up the ladder to the wharf and Baxter and Hall pulled him up. Billy took off his mask, his face blue with cold.

'You bloody idiot,' Dillon said.

'Well, I learned it from you. It was the seacocks, all four of them were wide open. I've closed them. It was hard going.'

Dillon said, 'The salvage people will need to pump her out. She'll float again.'

'Which leaves us with the problem of who did this.'

There was a pause, and then a quavery old drink-sodden voice said, 'I know, Mr Salter. I saw them, I heard them.'

It was Joe Baxter who said, 'Wally Brown. He dosses down in the packing cases.'

'And you heard them?' Harry demanded.

'Yes. One of them was called Murphy, but the one in charge was called Derry. That's what the other kept calling him and they spoke funny, Irish but not Irish.' He pointed at Dillon. 'Come to think of it, they talked like him.'

Ferguson said, 'Derry, and talks like you, Dillon. Northern Irish.'

Hannah said, 'Could that be Derry Gibson, the Red Hand of Ulster?'

'Back to haunt me. But why?' Dillon said.

'The Derry guy mentioned someone called Rossi?' old Wally put in.

The silence was astonishing. 'I'll kill him,' Harry said. 'I'll kill the bleeder.'

'No, you won't, Harry, or not yet,' Ferguson said. 'We'll go back to the Dark Man. Thank you, Mr Brown. That's been most helpful. Did you hear anything else?'

They all sat in the corner booth. Dora, the barmaid, provided tea and coffee. Harry and Billy Salter, Ferguson, Hannah and Dillon sat at the table. Baxter and Sam Hall leaned against the wall.

'They've declared open warfare,' Harry said.

'True.' Dillon nodded. 'But if you'll excuse me, Harry, the most important thing is that Rossi has struck a deal to deliver arms to Derry Gibson.' Wally Brown was devouring bacon and eggs at a corner table.

'So, according to Wally, Murphy was unhappy about sinking the boat and Derry threatened him. He said the deal with Rossi, the final arms shipment, would be the one he could use to take on the IRA again.'

'So what do you suggest?' Ferguson said.

'I wouldn't bother with the Baron or Rossi again. I'm going to have words with Pat Murphy.'

'You talk to that bastard, I'm going with you,' Harry Salter said.

Ferguson nodded. 'Try not to leave him floating in the Thames, Dillon.'

'Don't be silly, Charles, if he's been fronting in London for Derry Gibson and the Red Hand, he'll be far too valuable to waste.'

At South Audley Street, Marco sat with his father and told him what had happened. The Baron found it rather amusing.

'Oh, the great Harry Salter will not be pleased at all. But this other business. The *Mona Lisa*, the arms shipment. Is this wise?'

And Marco said exactly the right thing. 'It was one of the last things Kate Rashid organized, father. She'd worked with Derry Gibson before.' He pressed his point. 'He was, and still is, an admirer. He thought her a great lady – he told me so.'

'Really? He has taste, at least. This Spanish trawler, the *Mona Lisa*, how many in the crew?'

'The captain, a man called Juan Martino, and five crew members, all villains, of course.'

'And what will your part be in this?'

'On their way to Drumgoole, which is on the Down coast of Northern Ireland, they'll come close to the west coast of the Isle of Man. I've arranged with our contacts there to provide a motorboat to take me out to join her.'

'Is this strictly necessary, Marco?'

'No, but it gets me away from the office.'

The old man laughed. 'Go on, you rogue, but come back safe. I need you.'

The bar at the Orange George opened at nine in the morning, because it provided a full Irish breakfast. It was quiet enough when Dillon went in, Janet, the barmaid, reading a newspaper.

Dillon said, 'Tell Patrick I'd like a word.'

At that moment, the door at the end of the bar opened and Murphy appeared. He saw Dillon and a look of horror appeared on his face.

Dillon went round the bar. 'Patrick, my ould son, it's me, Sean Dillon.' He pushed him through to the hall. 'Do as you're told. Go on, unlock the back door,' which Murphy, terrified, did, and Harry and Billy crowded in. They shoved Murphy into the back parlour and closed the door.

Salter pushed him down into a chair at the table and slapped his face. 'You sodding bastard, you sank my boat.'

'Not me, Mr Salter, I swear.'

Billy pulled his uncle away. 'Let me get at him,' but Dillon intervened.

'No, leave it to me.' He took a Walther out of his pocket, then produced a Carswell silencer from the other and screwed it in place. 'This is much better. Hardly makes a sound. I'll start with his left elbow, then vary it. The right knee, maybe. That'll put him on sticks for six months.'

'Dear God, no.' Murphy really was terrified. 'What do you want?'

'Derry Gibson,' Dillon said. 'We'll forget about you sinking Mr Salter's *River Queen* for the moment. Tell me about Derry's deal with Rossi, the arms shipment.'

'Jesus, he'll kill me. He's a sadist, that one.'

'No, that's me,' Billy Salter said, and punched him twice in the stomach. 'Now speak up and tell Mr Dillon what he wants to know, or you'll end up in concrete in the new extension to the North Circular Road.'

And Murphy, aware that he was in truly bad company, talked.

At Ferguson's apartment, Murphy stayed outside in the car with Baxter and Hall, while Harry and Billy sat with Dillon and Ferguson, Hannah hanging around at the back.

'This could be a disaster,' Ferguson said. 'We all know the peace process has become a total shambles, the activities of IRA dissident groups prove that, but with this cargo of weapons, the Loyalists will be on a roll.'

Hannah said, 'We must put it into the hands of the Northern Ireland police, sir.'

'We can't afford to. If they make any kind of a move in the Drumgoole area,' Dillon said, 'Derry Gibson will know. It's not only his turf, his supporters have relatives in the police.'

143

'So what would you suggest?'

'Any stranger in the area would be a source of suspicion.'

'So what do we do, send in the SAS?'

'Nothing so official. The last time we did anything like this, we used a motor cruiser from Oban, from the RAF Air Sea Rescue base there. There's no reason we can't do it again. Book the boat, give me the right diving gear and enough Semtex, and I'll take it over by night and blow the *Mona Lisa* to hell.'

'On your own?' Ferguson asked.

'Why not? A totally black operation.'

'I don't like it, Dillon,' Hannah said. 'It's just not legal.'

'What about me, Dillon?' Billy said. 'Last time you played a gig like that, I went, too, and so did the Superintendent.'

'The Superintendent's not up for it because it offends her conscience, and you're not up for it because some months ago you had a bullet through the neck and two in the pelvis. As the Germans used to say when they took someone to prison camp, for you the war is over.'

'Stuff you, Dillon.'

Dillon turned to Ferguson. 'Do you want it done or not? There's an added benefit, you know. This could be just the thing we've been looking for to stir up von Berger, get him to make a mistake. We sink this boat, maybe something'll happen that'll give us a lead on that damned diary.'

Ferguson said, 'You're right, on both counts. Let's do it.' He turned to Hannah. 'Lock Murphy up at the St John's Wood safehouse. See he phones the Orange George and gives a reasonable excuse for his absence.'

'If that's how you want it, sir.'

'Dillon will give you a list of the weaponry and explosives he needs. The quartermaster will see to that. Book the Gulfstream with Squadron Leader Lacey. What do you think, Dillon? One o'clock tomorrow?'

'Fine by me, Charles.'

'Excellent. I'll see you there. I'm coming with you.'

Dillon said, 'What? You must be crazy.'

'Not as crazy as a man who thinks he can make a run from Oban to the Down coast on his own in what is usually a very rough sea. Haven't you ever heard of sleeping? I *am* something of a yachtsman, you know. I can actually navigate.'

'I surrender.' Dillon held up his hands.

At Farley Field the following day, Dillon reported to the quartermaster, a retired Guards sergeant major. He and Dillon had dealt together many times.

'Here you go, Mr Dillon. Three Walthers, three Uzi machine pistols, stun grenades and the Semtex you wanted. Ten-minute timing pencils, thirty-minute and one hour.'

'Excellent. What about diving equipment?'

'You'll find that on the boat at Oban, the *Highlander* – you've used it before. A couple of standard suits and fins, the usual extras.'

'Why two?'

'Always good to have back-up, sir.'

'Yes, I suppose so.'

At that moment, the Daimler arrived and Ferguson got out. His chauffeur took out a bag and delivered it to Parry, who took it up the steps and handed it to Sergeant Walters.

Dillon said, 'You look quite sporty, Charles. Corduroys, a sweater. Nice.'

'Very amusing,' Ferguson said. Then a Shogun drove up, Harry Salter at the wheel, Billy beside him. They got out, Billy in a black bomber jacket, a bag in one hand.

'Oh, now what in the hell is this?' Dillon asked.

'I'm coming along for the ride, that's what it is,' Billy said. 'You two are older guys. You could need some help.' He grinned.

145

Dillon looked at Ferguson, who shrugged. 'He was most insistent. I thought why not? He can go to hell in his own way.'

Harry said, 'Just bring him back in one piece, Dillon, because if you don't . . .'

'I get the picture, Harry.' Dillon turned to Billy, shaking his head. 'Old guy, huh? All right. Up you go then.'

He let Ferguson follow, then went up himself.

10

At the RAF Air Sea Rescue base at Oban, the commanding officer himself met them in view of Ferguson's rank. They were delivered in an unmarked car by two RAF sergeants named Smith and Brian.

'I think we met once before,' Dillon said.

Brian said, 'Not according to any office record, sir.' He grinned as they pulled in at the quay. 'You may recognize the *Highlander*. Two hundred yards out.'

'I can't say I'm impressed,' Ferguson said.

'You're not supposed to be,' Dillon told him, 'But it's got twin screws, a depth sounder, radar, automatic steering – and it does twenty-five knots.'

Sergeant Brian said, 'We've got a whale-boat to take your gear out.'

It took forty minutes, and when it was all stowed, Brian said, 'I don't know what you're up to, but good luck. You've got a first-class inflatable with an outboard motor. It should serve you well. We'll be getting back now.'

'Thanks,' Ferguson said.

The whaleboat departed and Dillon turned to Ferguson. 'Billy's been on board before. Let him show you around.

I'll contact Roper. See what his input is.'

Roper sat at his computer bank, examining the results of his latest hacking job into the Rashid computers.

Dillon said, 'What's the story on the *Mona Lisa?*'

'Operates from a small fishing port in northern Spain called San Miguel. The port's a hotbed for illegal transactions, but it's a bona fide Spanish deep-sea trawler, with a European licence to fish off Cornwall and Wales and in the Irish Sea.'

'What's its course?'

'According to its logged passage with the coastguard, she'll be close to the western coast of the Isle of Man tomorrow, then drift and fish towards the Down coast.'

'Very convenient. Anything else?'

'Not really. I'm sure, for instance, that you haven't the slightest interest in a Berger International flight into the Isle of Man, carrying one Marco Rossi.'

Dillon laughed. 'Well, imagine that.'

'If it's a sea voyage he's planning, he's in for a rough ride. Tomorrow and tomorrow night, there'll be rain squalls and high seas. You'll know you're out there!'

'Should be interesting.'

'Do you have a game plan, Sean?'

'Yeah, the game plan is to blow the hell out of the *Mona Lisa* and deposit two million quid's worth of arms on the floor of the Irish Sea.'

'What about the crew? I've got a Captain Martino listed here and five others: Gomez, Fabio, Arturo somebody, an Enrico, a Sancho. You're going to kill them all, Sean?'

'Why not? They're a reasonable facsimile of scum. They've run everything from heroin to human beings, I'm told, and now arms. They shouldn't have joined if they didn't want the risk.'

148

'Fine by me. I'll stay in touch. Speak to you tomorrow.'

'Good, but stay on the Berger case. I'm convinced Rossi was responsible for Sara Hesser's death.'

'I'll see what I can do.'

Oban was enveloped in mist and rain. Beyond Kerrera, the waters looked disturbed in the Firth of Lorn, and clouds draped across the mountain tops.

'I've said it before,' Billy moaned. 'What a bloody awful place. I mean, it rains all the bleeding time.'

'No, Billy, it rains six days a week.' Dillon turned to Ferguson. 'Am I right, General?'

'You usually are, Dillon.'

'Good. Please join me in the wheelhouse.'

There was a flap to one side of the instrument panel and he pressed a button. Inside was a fuse box and some clips screwed into place. He opened one of the weapons bags, took out a Browning with a twenty-round magazine protruding from its butt. He clipped it into place and added a Walther in the other clips.

'Ace in the hole.' He closed the flap.

'My goodness, you do mean business,' Ferguson said.

'I always did, Charles. Now let's go ashore and eat.'

The early darkness of the far north was against them and he turned on the deck lights, then they coasted to the front at Oban in the inflatable and tied up. A pub close by offered food, and they went in. There was a meat and potato pie on the menu, which they all ordered.

'I'll have a large Scotch, Dillon. Billy, what about you?'

'Billy doesn't drink,' Dillon told Ferguson.

'I hate the taste of booze,' Billy said.

'It's all in the Bible: wine is a mocker, strong drink raging,' Dillon said.

'Well, you still do it.'

'True.' Dillon swallowed his Bushmills. 'What's more, I'll have another.'

'I despair of you, Dillon,' Ferguson said, and then the pies arrived and killed conversation for a while.

Later, back on the *Highlander*, they sat on the stern deck under the canvas awning, rain bouncing off. Ferguson said, 'So, what's the plan?'

'Roper tells me the *Mona Lisa's* due off the west coast of the Isle of Man tomorrow. And guess who's flying up there in a Berger International plane? Marco Rossi.'

'You didn't tell me,' Ferguson said.

'I've been saving it up for you. I think it means he fancies a passage by night to Drumgoole.'

'That could very well be. When we get there, what do you intend?'

'I told Roper, I'll blow the damn boat up, and don't ask me what about the crew. They're all what the Italians would call *animali*. With any luck, Rossi could even be on board.'

'You really are yourself alone, Dillon. I wonder about Derry Gibson.'

'Wonder what?'

'He could give us a lot of trouble. This Red Hand of Ulster – where do they get their absurd names from?'

'It's their simple Irish minds, Charles. I'd have thought you'd have recognized that, your sainted mother being a Cork woman.'

'All right, I take your point. But this Derry Gibson thing. It could lead to greater civil war than ever, Catholics and Protestants.'

'What would you like me to do? Shoot Gibson?'

'It wouldn't be a bad idea.'

'That's good,' Billy said. 'He's Wyatt Earp, I'm Doc Holliday, and you'd like Derry Gibson and Rossi standing up in coffins in the undertaker's window, like in Dodge City, hands folded, eyes closed.'

'You know something, Billy? I couldn't have put it better myself.' Ferguson got up. 'It's me for an early night. I'll see you in the morning. I just have one question. Getting in close to the Drumgoole area – won't the locals wonder who we are?'

'Not if we take out the nets that are in the hold and drape them around the deck. There are lots of fishing boats off the Down coast.'

'Good enough,' Ferguson said, and went below.

Billy said, 'He's such a gent, but you know what? I reckon he's harder than Harry, and that's saying something.'

'He's the kind of man who got us the Empire in the first place,' Dillon said. 'Mind you, he's right about Derry Gibson. I'll give it some thought.'

'You mean you'd consider knocking him off?'

'Why not? I've killed for worse reasons. I once saved his life, you know. We were in a sewer in Londonderry, being hunted by Brit paratroopers, even though we were on different sides. I told him then to keep running and not come back, or I'd kill him.'

'And now?'

'Looks like he's come back. Come on, let's go to bed,' and Dillon led the way below.

The following morning, with rain drifting in, Ferguson went up on deck and discovered Dillon swimming in the sea, sporting with two seals, Billy leaning on the rail, watching.

'He's mad,' Billy said.

'Yes, I've been aware of that for some years.'

'I mean, talk about freeze your balls off.'

Dillon swam to the ladder and hauled himself up. 'The grand appetite it gives you, Charles.' The ship-to-shore radio crackled in the wheelhouse. 'Take that, Charles, it could be Roper. I'll get dressed.'

It was Roper. 'Ah, it's you, General. Just updating you. Rossi's plane lands at Ronaldsway on the Isle of Man at eleven this morning. The *Mona Lisa* is five miles out and scheduled to move to the Down coastal area later this afternoon. The weather isn't good, so I'd say it wouldn't be in the Drumgoole area until tonight. I don't know. The weather makes it uncertain.'

'Right. Thanks, Roper.'

He turned as Dillon entered the wheelhouse and filled him in. Dillon had a look at the chart. 'I've done this kind of run before, so I know what I'm doing, but the weather stinks. Look at it, Charles.'

The whole of Oban was draped in mist. 'Bleeding awful,' Billy said.

'All right.' Dillon nodded. 'Let's allow for him landing at eleven, being driven across the island, and then some sort of boat running him five miles out to the *Mona Lisa*. It's two o'clock at the earliest before he boards and she turns for Ulster, but with that weather . . .' He shook his head. 'What do you think, Charles?'

'Three o'clock at the earliest.'

'All right. We'll leave at two, then. For the moment, let's get back ashore for a full Scots breakfast . . . and by the look of it, seasick pills for Billy.'

The flights from London to Ronaldsway had been bad enough. Rossi, the ex-Tornado pilot, always liked to take over the controls for a while, but it was rough and the cross winds at the airport had been treacherous, although he'd managed the landing himself. A local Rashid employee met him with a car and took him across the island to a small village, where a motor cruiser waited.

It had a crew of two and set out to sea immediately, pushing out from the shelter of a small pier into the rough waves, obscured by fog. It took them an hour to find the *Mona Lisa*. They pulled alongside the Spanish trawler, its nets draped high over the stern. The two ships collided twice, and men leaned over with grappling lines. Rossi took his chance and jumped over to the other boat. He turned and waved to the motor cruiser, the captain waved back and then he motored away.

Three or four men at the rail eyed Rossi up and down. He ignored them and went towards the wheelhouse. The door opened and a man emerged in a reefer coat and seaman's cap, heavily unshaven, an unlit cigarette in the corner of his mouth.

By any estimate, he would have been termed a nasty piece of work. He looked Rossi over with a kind of contempt. 'I'm Martino, the captain.'

'And I'm Marco Rossi, your boss.'

A couple of the men laughed and Martino lit his cigarette. 'Should I be impressed?'

Rossi reached, grabbed his left ear, his thumb well inside, and produced his Walther and rammed it hard under the chin.

'Now, you have the option of continuing to be employed by Rashid and make a lot of money, or I blow your brains out now, up through the mouth and into the brain. Explodes the back of the skull. Very messy.'

Martino tried to smile. 'Eh, *Señor*, there's a mistake here.'

'Not mine, yours. Screw with me and you're finished. Do we understand each other?'

'Perfectly, *Senor.*'

'Good. Then let's get on with it.'

He walked into the wheelhouse and the crew looked at Martino, who nodded, so they went about their tasks.

* * *

Around the middle of the afternoon the *Highlander* was ploughing through a turbulent sea, down from Oban, a couple of miles off the Isle of Man into the Irish Sea. Dillon was at the wheel, Billy at the chart table and Ferguson below.

The mist was so heavy, the driving rain so intense, that it was more like evening, a kind of early darkness, and Dillon could see one of the Irish ferries, red-and-green navigational lights already visible.

Ferguson came into the wheelhouse, with three mugs of tea on a tray. He put the tray down on the table and looked at the chart, then switched the ship-to-shore radio to weather and listened.

'It's going to get worse before it gets better. Better let me have the wheel, Dillon.'

Dillon didn't even argue. Ferguson altered course a couple of points, then increased his speed, racing the heavy weather that threatened from the east. The waves grew rougher.

'Jesus,' Billy said. 'I'm scared to death.'

'No need, Billy, he knows what he's doing. I'll go down to the galley and make some bacon sandwiches.'

'Not for me. I could throw up now.'

'Take another couple of pills,' Dillon said, and went below.

He came back half an hour later with sandwiches on a plate and found Ferguson alone.

'What happened to the boy wonder?'

'Took a couple of pills and retired to lie down. I say, those smell good.'

'Help yourself.'

Ferguson put the steering on automatic and took a bacon sandwich. Dillon splashed whiskey into two plastic cups and they ate together in companionable silence. It was getting really dark now, far earlier than normal, only a slight phosphorescence shining from the sea.

'You seem at home,' Dillon said.

'I always liked the sea, from boyhood. The West Sussex coast, down to the Isle of Wight, the Solent. Loved it.' He drank the whiskey. 'I'll have the other half.'

He helped himself to another sandwich. 'That Browning with the twenty-shot magazine you've put in the flap there. It took me back.'

'Really?'

'Yes. In nineteen seventy-three, I took extended leave. I was an acting major then. Done rather well for my age. I did the Atlantic run single-handed, Portsmouth to Long Island. It had to be Long Island, because I had an old uncle living there. He was a general too. The American connection in my family.'

'A remarkable achievement,' Dillon said.

'Therapy, Dillon, therapy.' He finished the last sandwich and took the wheel again.

'What for?'

'Well, I'd been shot in the shoulder, but it was more than that. It was psychological. Coming to terms with what I was capable of.'

Dillon poured two more whiskeys. 'And what was that?'

'I was never SAS, Dillon. What you've never known was that I served with Code Nine Intelligence.'

He had just named one of the most infamous army units involved in the underground fight with the IRA.

'Jesus,' Dillon said.

'It was a hell of a way to earn a living in Londonderry in nineteen seventy-three, but there I was. Thirty years old, Oxford, Sandhurst, Malaya, Communist rebels in the Yemen, Eoka in Cyprus, and then along came Ireland. I couldn't wait to switch from the Grenadier Guards to counter-insurgency work.'

'You wanted the smell of powder again?'

'Of war, Dillon. I'd been engaged for three years, a lovely girl called Mary. From an army family, only she could never see the point. Mind you, she hung in there until Cork Street.'

He was talking as if he was alone, taking some kind of solitary journey into the past.

'Cork Street?' Dillon said. 'What was that?'

'That was where I earned the Military Cross, Dillon, one of those they handed out in Northern Ireland for unspecified reasons.'

Dillon said softly, 'And what would that be, Charles?'

'Well, I was link man between two safehouses run by the SAS. One night, I was doing a run quite late. As we discovered later, my cover had been blown. Going through Cork Street down by the docks, I'd a car on my tail, then another came out of a side street and turned to block me.'

'Just a minute,' Dillon said. 'July, 'Seventy-three, Derry – the Cork Street massacre, that's what they called it. The SAS took out five Provos. A hell of a thing.'

'No, they didn't. *I* took out five Provos.'

It was only then that Dillon was aware of a slight noise. He turned and found the door half open and Billy standing there.

Ferguson glanced over his shoulder, 'Come in, Billy. Yes, Dillon, the second car blocked me, and the one in the rear was right up my backside. There were three Provos in front, two at my back. They just shouted. "Out, out, you Brit bastard." It always seemed ironic, being half-Irish. It's the posh voice, you see.'

'So what did you do?'

'I had what you've got in there, a Browning with a twenty-round magazine, on the left-hand seat. One man wrenched open the driver's door, so I shot him between the eyes, then shot his two friends through the door. I was using hollow-point cartridges. Devastating.'

'And?'

'The two men in the rear car scrambled to get out. One of them fired wildly and was lucky. Hit me in the left shoulder. I riddled the car, a kind of reflex, killed him and the driver. Then I drove away, and made it to one of the safehouses, where the SAS patched me up and got me out the following morning.'

'Jesus,' Billy said. 'You killed five.'

'All gone to that great IRA heaven in the sky, Billy, and the doctors put me together again and my masters gave me the Military Cross – had to, really. The loss of five members of the Londonderry Brigade was so mortifying that the Provos put it about as another SAS atrocity, and in the mythology of Irish Republicanism, that's where it remains.'

It was Dillon who sensed more. 'So what happened afterwards?'

'Oh, I got a call to pick up the medal from Her Majesty at Buckingham Palace, and I asked Mary to go with me. She'd visited me in the hospital, and naturally wanted to know how I'd come to be there, so I told her.'

'And what happened?'

'She sent the engagement ring back, and a letter explaining that she couldn't possibly marry a man who'd killed five people.'

'Well, damn her eyes,' Billy said.

'That's one point of view. So I went to the Palace on my own. A nasty, wet day it was, too. The Regiment was proud of me. Gave me leave.'

'Which you used to sail to Long Island. You thought a hard sea voyage would blow the cobwebs away?' Dillon said.

'Something like that.'

'But in the end, you were still the man who shot five men dead, right?'

'That's right.'

'General, they asked for it and they got it,' Billy said.

157

'True, Billy, I did my duty and it cost me Mary.' He said to Dillon, 'God knows why I bothered to tell you after all these years. I think I'm getting maudlin in my old age. Take the wheel and I'll go and have a rest,' and he went out.

Billy said, 'My God, I said he was harder than Harry, but I never dreamed he was capable of a thing like that.'

'Oh, he probably killed before in all those rotten little wars, Billy. Cork Street was his spectacular.' He lit a cigarette. 'Remember what I told you before, about the people who take care of the bad things that ordinary folk find impossible to handle? The soldiers? I'm a soldier, whether people approve of me or not, and so are you, and then we get Charles Ferguson, a decent honourable man who could have been a banker or a lawyer. Instead he's spent his life saving his country.'

Behind them, Ferguson said from the doorway, 'That's nice of you, Dillon, but don't let's overdo it, and as far as the steering goes, I'd say a couple of points west.'

In Drumgoole, in the back room of the pub, Derry Gibson ate bacon and eggs served by the local publican, one Keith Adair, his right-hand man in the little port.

'Is there anything else I can get you?' Adair asked.

'No, this is grand. It's the weather I don't like. It's bad out there and getting worse. I'd hoped the *Mona Lisa* could come into the jetty by the old stone quarry. If it gets worse, the skipper will have to drop his hook out in the bay.'

'That'll make it more difficult to unload, Derry. Mind you, plenty of local fishermen have signed up for that.'

'Well, they would, wouldn't they? What about the local peelers?'

'They've closed the police station down, Derry. Some trouble up in Castleton, so they've gone up there to help out.'

'Excellent. They know which side their bread's buttered on.'

At that moment, the phone sounded and Adair passed it to him.

'Mr Gibson, it's Janet from the Orange George.'

'I know who you are, Janet. What's the problem?'

'Well, I was wondering if you knew where Patrick is? It's been a couple of days. He phoned once and said his Uncle Arthur had died unexpectedly and I was to carry on running the pub, only we got cut off and I've got bills coming in and I can't write the cheques, so I thought I'd speak to you, knowing you're the real owner.'

'Just a minute,' Derry told her. 'He doesn't have an Uncle Arthur.'

'Well, that's what he said.'

And years of bad living made Derry Gibson sit up very straight. He nodded to Adair and switched the phone to speaker.

'When did you last see him, Janet?'

'Later in the morning when you went off for the plane to Belfast. I was doing breakfasts. This small man came in. Black bomber jacket, jeans, and that funny kind of fair hair, almost white. He asked for Patrick, and at that moment Patrick came in by the rear door.'

'And what happened?'

'Well, the little guy said, "Patrick, my old son, it's me, Sean Dillon." He had one of those Belfast accents like yours, Mr Gibson.'

Derry Gibson went cold. 'And what happened?'

'That was it. Nothing until the phone call, and then today, I was talking to that old Kelly guy who sells the newspapers outside, and he said he was surprised to see Patrick getting in a Shogun with three guys, because he knew two of them well, Harry Salter and his nephew, Billy. Big gangsters.'

It was enough. Derry Gibson said, 'There's a lot going on here you don't know about, Janet. Just keep things going. If you look in the right-hand top drawer of Patrick's desk, you'll find a company credit card. Use it to pay bills. I'll be in touch.'

He switched off and turned to Adair. 'Sean Dillon and those Salter guys. That means Ferguson.'

'Jesus, they'll have squeezed Murphy dry,' Adair said. 'We're up the creek.'

'No, not the way Ferguson and Dillon work.' Gibson's face was hard. 'Every job is a black operation to them. No police, no SAS, just Dillon and whatever he comes up with. It's always been the way he plays the game.'

'Which means?'

Gibson laughed and it was as if he was enjoying it. 'He's at sea already, homing on the *Mona Lisa*.'

'So what do we do?'

'Give him a welcome, his last on this earth. I'll phone Rossi and let him know what to expect.'

On the bridge of the *Mona Lisa*, Martino was at the wheel, Rossi at one side, the boat pounding through heavy weather as darkness descended. The ship-to-shore sounded, and Martino answered. He turned to Rossi.

'It's for you.'

Rossi took it and listened to what Gibson had to say. 'In Sean Dillon's hands, Murphy will spill his guts.' Rossi felt strangely calm, not in the least put out. 'Dillon really is a piece of work.'

'So what do we do?'

'Well, it's up to the captain in this weather. If he can come in and make the jetty, fine,' Gibson said. 'If it's too rough, drop the anchor in the bay. I'll have suitable back-up here in Drumgoole, but you break out your weapons on board and keep a weather eye out for any likely craft.'

'You really think Dillon is actually at sea?'

'I wouldn't be surprised. He and Ferguson will see the *Mona Lisa* as a prime target and they'll do it their way. Look, all this rubbish about Northern Ireland and peace initiatives. It's crap, because the IRA and Sinn Fein have abused the system, and the British government has let them do it. I'm a good Orange Prod and I know it, because someone like Ferguson classes me with the IRA.'

'So what are you saying?

'That Ferguson doesn't play by the rules, because he knows the justice system doesn't work. That's why he has Sean Dillon. He'll come in the hard way.'

He hung up.

Rossi stood there thinking, and turned to Martino.

'Break out the weapons and tell everyone to keep watch. Any other boat, we approach with caution.'

'Why, *Señor*?'

Rossi smiled grimly. 'We're about to have company, Captain.'

11

Dillon spoke to Roper as the *Highlander* ploughed through heavy seas towards the Northern Irish coast.

'It's rough,' Dillon said. 'And getting rougher.'

'If the *Mona Lisa*'s off Drumgoole, try and make it to the entrance to the bay by the jetty to the old quarry. There's a trough. Four hundred feet.'

'Thanks, that's helpful.'

'And please watch it. Things are really moving out there. Don't, for God's sake, consider only the great Sean Dillon and his mission to save the world.'

The voice crackled over the ship-to-shore radio, and Dillon turned to Ferguson and Billy, who were listening.

He said, 'Message received and understood, Roper. We who are about to die salute you, only I don't plan to die just yet. This weather might be just what we need. Over and out.'

Dillon took a bottle of Lamb's Navy Rum out of the flare drawer, pulled the cork and swallowed deep. He passed the bottle to Ferguson. 'You're going to need it, Charles.'

Ferguson didn't hesitate. He drank, wiped the neck and offered the bottle to Billy, who said, 'No, I'll manage. I'm so bleeding scared I don't feel seasick any more.'

Ferguson was at the wheel, which responded surprisingly well. 'What happens now?' he demanded.

Dillon leaned over the chart table. 'I don't know. If the *Mona Lisa* ties up at that jetty, fine. If it puts its anchor down in the bay, I'll go in underwater with Semtex and timer pencils. An in-and-out job. Blow the bottom out of her, and down she goes.'

'It won't be too deep if she's at the jetty.'

'We'll have to see. The bay would be better. There'll be a hell of a lot of confusion there. God help all the small harbour craft, the fishing boats.'

'So that's it then?' Ferguson said.

'That's exactly it, Charles.' Dillon smiled. 'We're totally in the hands of the weather. I'll go below and get into my wetsuit.'

'Me, too,' Billy said.

'Not in a million years. You can run the inflatable, take me close, but that's it. Open the weapons bag and arm up, Billy, I won't be long,' and he went below.

In Drumgoole harbour, the scene was total confusion, the wind coming in off the Irish Sea and gusting to storm force. Smaller craft were already being torn from their moorings and smashed against the harbour walls. Other craft were breaking free and being sucked out into the bay on the other side of the jetty. In the midst of all this, the *Mona Lisa* emerged, her deck lights on, a kind of ghost ship, very old-fashioned, her superstructure high, Martino and Rossi way up on the bridge.

Derry Gibson's voice came over the ship-to-shore. 'Don't come in, you'll smash up against the old jetty. Drop your hook, and if you're lucky you'll find it about sixty or seventy feet, but there's a trough of four hundred feet, I can't help you there.'

Rossi said, 'No news of our friends?'

'Jesus, Marco, if they're out there, they'll be as much in harm's way as the rest of us. I'll join you. We've got a RNLI inshore inflatable lifeboat here. They can handle most things. I'll see you.'

Way out in the bay, the *Highlander* hove to and Ferguson tossed out a sea anchor. Dillon, in his wetsuit, looked out towards the distant *Mona Lisa* through night binoculars. Billy was using another pair.

'Dillon, there are boats floating out of the harbour, bouncing off the *Mona Lisa*'s hull like rubber balls.'

'Only they're splintering, Billy. I've counted at least three in a sinking condition, but the *Mona Lisa*'s got an anchor chain down.'

Dillon put the weapons bag on the chart table, took out an arm holster, a Browning with the same twenty-round magazine in it as the hidden one, put it on, then crossed a weapon bag over his shoulder, took out three Semtex blocks and inserted ten-minute pencil timers. He slipped an inflatable belt around his waist.

'Nothing bulletproof?' Ferguson said.

'A titanium waistcoat under my wetsuit, Charles, the best I can afford.'

'What do you want me to do?'

'Cross her stern. We'll drift in like the other boats. I'll go over and climb the anchor line.'

'With luck?'

'Oh, we all need that, Charles.'

'And me?' Billy asked.

'When I hopefully survive long enough to jump over the rail, you may need to bring the inflatable in and pick me up. Turn it on and the engine goes to forty knots. I'll send a flare up.'

'Not in this weather,' Ferguson said.

A huge cross-wind turned them half over, and they all staggered and grabbed. Billy said, 'You can't, Dillon, it's madness.'

Dillon put an arm around him. 'You're a great guy, Billy, but I don't care any more. I'm going to blow the hell out of that boat and everybody on it, whether that's Gibson, Rossi – or even me,' and he said it with great deliberation.

The *Mona Lisa* bucked on its anchor as one craft after another crashed against it. There was total confusion on deck; the crew, who had previously been at the ready with their AK47s, now panicked as the boat rolled from side to side.

The *Highlander* eased forward and Dillon slipped over the side as they passed the stern of the *Mona Lisa*. The waves sucked him in, tossed him over and he grabbed the anchor line. He hung there, his rubber gloves giving him a grip as the *Highlander* sped away.

He started to haul himself up, waves washing over him, and then reached the hole at the top and slid in through to the stern. There were two of the crew there, Fabio and Gomez, utterly confused by the waves breaking over the rails, clutching their AK47s.

They saw Dillon get to his knees, and then he pulled out the Browning and shot both of them in the head.

High up on the bridge, it was Derry Gibson who recognized the sound for what it was. 'He's here, the bastard's here.'

'Who is?' Martino asked.

'Dillon, you miserable idiot.'

Gibson went out, looked down, and saw Fabio and Gomez rolling in the scuppers.

'There you are.'

Martino, at his side, was horrified. 'I can't believe it.'

At that moment, Arturo and Enrico came round the central area on the port side, grabbing for the rail in the heavy sea, and Dillon, crouched in the stern, shot them both.

He moved forward on the port side, heavy seas breaking over him, reached the prow of the boat, heaved the hatch back on the engine room, took out the three blocks of Semtex with the timer pencils and dropped them in.

Bullets ripped up the decks beside him. He turned and found the man, Sancho, standing there, firing an AK47, and up high on the wheelhouse deck, Martino, Rossi and Gibson at the rail. He seemed to be facing an inevitable death, and then bullets cut across the decks, Martino was hurled back, and Sancho went down. Gibson ducked and ran away. Dillon looked over and saw Billy at the wheel of the inflatable, Ferguson standing up and spraying the *Mona Lisa* with the Browning from the wheelhouse.

Dillon ran and vaulted over the rail, and as the inflatable went by, grabbed a line and was hauled away.

'Out, out, out,' Gibson called to Rossi.

He went down the side ladder, ended up in the bouncing inflatable and had the engine revving as Rossi joined him. A moment only, and they sped away through the heavy sea. A moment later, the *Highlander's* inflatable appeared out of the gloom, Ferguson standing up with the Browning, Dillon trailing behind. Ferguson had no chance to fire; they were away.

Rossi said, 'Ferguson, young Salter.'

'And Dillon,' Gibson said.

Behind them, the three Semtex blocks Dillon had dropped into the engine room exploded one after the other. The *Mona Lisa* simply blew apart. Parts of her superstructure flew up and then rained down into the storm below. The boat tilted, the stern rose, the *Mona Lisa* slid over the edge of the trough and went all the way down. There was another muffled explosion, an enormous convulsion to the already-disturbed sea surface, boats thrown all over the place, and then a strange calm. The wind dropped just then, only the rain continued, hard and forceful. The inflatable reached the *Highlander* and drifted against the side.

Dillon pulled himself up the ladder, paused and turned. 'You must have been fantastic when you were young, Charles, because you are indescribable now.'

'Don't forget, Billy, and don't try to butter me up, Dillon. Just get on board and let's turn for Oban. We've done what we came here for.'

'Except that Marco Rossi and Derry Gibson are left standing.'

'We'll sort them another day.'

Rossi phoned his father. 'I'll be back tomorrow. I want out of this damned country.'

'Why? What happened?'

Rossi explained, and his father actually found it funny. 'Ferguson, at his age. You must admit, Marco, it's rather admirable.'

'Well, I've got a boat with two million pounds of weaponry sent down to the bottom by your *admirable* Ferguson.'

'Come home and we'll discuss it.'

Afterwards, the Baron sat, smoking a cigarette and sipping a large brandy, and he was actually smiling.

The *Highlander* ploughed on, Ferguson at the wheel. Billy appeared with the bacon sandwiches.

'I'll tell you what, you old bastard, you were great back there. Harry won't believe it when I tell him.'

'You didn't do badly yourself, Billy.'

Dillon came in, now changed, in jeans and a shirt. Ferguson said, 'I'll say it now. You were totally mad. Frankly, Dillon, you've got a death wish.'

'You're right, General, but it got the job done.'

'I think you should visit Professor Susan Haden-Taylor again.'

'No, she's washed her hands of me, and so has God. For the moment, we've succeeded in what we set out to achieve.

167

Fewer arms for the conflict in Northern Ireland – and I'll be willing to bet we've stirred up a hornet's nest with Rossi and von Berger. Now, we wait and see where it leads – with luck, to the diary. By the way, I've phoned Harry, told him his nephew is still in the land of the living.'

'Thanks very much, Dillon,' Billy said.

'That's all right, Billy, he worries about you. Now, would it be all right if *I* had a bacon sandwich?'

12

In Drumgoole there was a certain amount of chaos, but Northern Ireland had been used to chaos for almost thirty-five years. Nevertheless, Derry Gibson was in the market to move on.

'We'll have the peelers all over the place for a while,' he said to Rossi in the pub after the *Mona Lisa* went down. 'I'll lie low.' He was having a whiskey, and shook his head as he drank it down. 'Sean Dillon – what a bastard he is, and Ferguson.'

'Yes, you should never underestimate your opponent. I'll be out of this pesthole first thing in the morning. As far as I'm concerned, you can give Northern Ireland back to the Indians.'

'I think you're being a bit rough.'

'I could be a damn sight rougher. I could point out, for instance, that you haven't paid anything on the *Mona Lisa* contract. She's gone down and Rashid doesn't get a penny.'

'What happened, happened, Rossi. You were screwed and I was screwed. By Dillon and Ferguson.'

'Yes, I've been thinking about that. It's time we did something about Dillon and Ferguson.'

'Can I help?'

'Well, it would be a way of writing off your debt.' He thought for a moment. 'Where do you think Murphy is?'

'Ferguson's got him in some safehouse,' said Gibson. 'The only reason those bastards were here was because Murphy talked.'

'Yes. Tell you what, Gibson. Don't go back to the Orange George. Call that woman, Janet, and tell her she's in charge for a little while more.'

'And where do I stay?'

'In one of our staff flats on South Audley Street.'

'Until when?'

'Until I've worked out how I'm going to do it.'

'Do what? Something with Dillon?'

'Eventually, but not yet. First, I think it'll be Ferguson, the great man himself.'

Gibson was delighted. 'What in the hell are you up to?'

'You'll have to wait, Derry. I'll let you know in good time.'

He lit a cigarette. Derry said, 'You're enjoying all this. You should have been crushed by the loss of the *Mona Lisa*. Instead, you don't give a stuff. Two million.'

'It's only money, Derry, and money is only a medium of exchange. No, the game's the thing.'

'That sounds like Shakespeare.'

'Close. But it's what you and me are all about, as well as Dillon, Ferguson, even the Salters. It's the game that makes you feel alive. It's worth everything.'

As soon as he got back to London, Ferguson requested a meeting with the Prime Minister, on a one-to-one basis, no other security people present, not even Scotland Yard. When he was ushered into the Prime Minister's study, he found him signing various documents for the Foreign Secretary, who had never approved of Ferguson.

'I've heard a rumour you've been up to some kind of nonsense again, General,' he said.

'Me, Foreign Secretary? Can't imagine what. I've been up to my neck in things at the Ministry of Defence for the past few days.'

'Really?' the Foreign Secretary said dryly.

The Prime Minister passed across the documents. 'There you go. No feuding, you two, you're both far too important.'

'Pax,' Ferguson said; the Foreign Secretary smiled reluctantly and departed.

The Prime Minister said, 'Right, General, you'd better sit down and tell me the worst.'

Afterwards he said, 'That's the deepest black operation I've ever heard of. No wonder you didn't want anyone else present. There are rumours, of course, already. God help us if this kind of thing ever reached the ears of the public.'

'It's too fantastic. No one would believe it.'

The Prime Minister nodded. 'When I won my election I was presented with knowledge of your department, a secret passed from one PM to another about an organization responding only to the PM's will. It made me feel uneasy, and yet on so many occasions, you, Dillon and company, have saved the day. The peace process in Northern Ireland is in tatters, but we're still trying. If the Red Hand of Ulster had got hold of the *Mona Lisa*'s weaponry, it could have been civil war.'

'Exactly, sir.'

'So, a good job well done. There's only one thing that bothers me. Dillon and young Salter, I can understand, but you, Charles? Exchanging shot for shot at your age? It's not only undignified, it's also damned dangerous. You've got your medals, Charles. No more sorties going into harm's way, all right?'

'I promise, Prime Minister.'

'Yes, well, I think I'm going to make sure. You know about the Omega programme, don't you, Charles?'

'Yes, sir, it's an implant containing a computer chip that tracks a person's whereabouts.'

'Exactly. I've got it. So do the cabinet ministers. And I've decided you should have it, too.'

'Must I, Prime Minister?'

'Yes, Charles, you're too valuable to lose.' He picked up a card and handed it over. 'Professor Henry Merriman, Harley Street. Be there at nine o'clock tomorrow morning. It only takes half an hour or so. Doesn't hurt.'

'Would Dillon be a candidate?'

'No. It's only for very senior political figures – and, frankly, Charles, I don't think I want to know where Dillon is all the time.'

'Two American Presidents owe him their lives.'

'I'm aware of that.'

'And yet Dillon has no medals at all.'

'Yes, life can be a bitch, General.'

Ferguson was silent. 'Yes, well, I will, of course, present myself at the Harley Street clinic, as you wish, Prime Minister.'

He moved to the door, and the Prime Minister said, 'And von Berger, Charles, don't forget von Berger.'

Ferguson turned and said, 'Sir?'

'Can't have him threatening the President and me. It won't do. Bring him down, Charles, any way it takes.'

'Of course, sir.' Ferguson brushed past the aide, went downstairs and out to the Daimler, where Dillon and Hannah waited.

Dillon moved to one of the jump seats and closed the glass partition. 'How did it go?'

Ferguson told them, and Hannah said, 'I think Omega is a good idea and you *are* important.'

'A damn sight more important than most of the half-baked cabinet ministers around at the moment,' Dillon said.

'Why, thank you, Dillon.'

'It's a fact of life. I won't remind you of how many years you've been around in the intelligence game, but I can't think of anyone else in the Western world with your experience.'

'You should be my press agent.'

'Glad to. So, von Berger – did he come up?'

'The PM was explicit. Bring him down.'

'Easier said than done. Unless you'd like me to shoot him for you?'

Hannah said, 'For God's sake, Dillon.'

He opened the side window and lit a cigarette. 'As I've said before, the Almighty has got little to do with it. I could take out Rossi quite cheerfully. Would that be okay?'

'You're being stupid.'

Ferguson said, 'Cut it out, you two. What about Rossi's movements, Superintendent?'

'He left Belfast this morning.'

Ferguson turned to Dillon. 'Call Roper. See if he's got anything.'

Roper had, of course. 'Landed at Gatwick, one pilot, two passengers.'

'You need two pilots for those things, it's the law.'

'Of course, but Marco Rossi's fully rated, he was the other one.'

'Who was the passenger?'

'One Charles Mackenzie, carrying a UK passport issued in Northern Ireland, an accountant apparently.'

'Apparently?'

'I went into the new visual system they have at check-in now and had a look at him. Derry Gibson.'

'I might have known.'

'You don't know anything, Sean. What he's doing here, for instance. Neither of them have any reason to be pleased with you.'

'So I should be looking over my shoulder?'

'He *is* Red Hand of Ulster, old son.'

'I'm frightened to death, Roper,' Dillon said. 'Goodbye.'

'What was that all about?' Ferguson asked.

Dillon told him.

'Hmm,' Ferguson said. 'You know, I've been thinking. Blowing up that ship was good, but why should we wait for them to make the next move? Why not stay on the offensive? We should know more about von Berger's set-up in Germany. Schloss Adler, Neustadt, the dark place, whatever the hell they call it.' He turned to Hannah. 'Have a word with Roper, ask him to do a quick computer analysis of the area. See if we've got any intelligence sources there. Tell him to meet us at that restaurant of Salter's, Harry's Place. We'll have a meal and listen to what he has to say. We'll call at the Dark Man first.'

Two car lengths back, Newton and Cook followed.

It was early evening, the Dark Man quiet, Salter and Billy as usual in the corner booth, Joe Baxter and Sam Hall hanging around, when Ferguson and the others walked in.

Harry said, 'This is a nice surprise, general, sit down, all of you.' He said to Dillon, 'And you listened to me – brought Billy back in one piece.'

'After covering himself with glory.'

'No, that was the general,' Billy said.

Harry turned to Dillon. 'And you, of course, did the usual.'

'More or less.'

'So what gives?'

'Rossi flew in from Belfast this morning, with a passenger named Charles Mackenzie on his passport.'

'But in fact, Derry Gibson, according to Roper,' Hannah put in.

Harry said, 'And what would that bastard be doing here?'

'Yes, that's the thing,' Ferguson said.

'Well, I'd say it's bleeding obvious,' Billy put in. 'He's out for you, Dillon.'

Dillon lit a cigarette. 'He could be out for any one of us.'

'Well, just let him try,' Harry said. 'He sank my boat. I'll have him for that.'

'The important thing is to find out what the Baron and Rossi plan to do next,' said Ferguson. 'I've got Roper doing one of his searches on von Berger's place in Germany. I suggested he meet us at your restaurant, Harry, if that suits you.'

'Absolutely.'

Newton phoned Rossi again. 'We've followed them to this restaurant in Wapping, Harry's Place. They've gone in, and Roper's turned up in his wheelchair.'

'Stay there.' Rossi turned to the Baron.

'Interesting,' von Berger said, and then, with a twinkle in his eye, 'I'll tell you what, Marco, let's go meet them. Oh! And go and get Mr Gibson. We'll all go together. We'll stir the pot! Won't that be amusing?'

'Infinitely,' Marco said.

Harry's Place was another of Salter's warehouse conversions on Hangman's Wharf. The whole place had been revitalized, its brickwork cleaned, new windows in mahogany. There was always a queue, mainly of young people trying to get into the bar, which had become a smart place to be seen. Steps had been added to make the entrance more imposing, and there was a ramp beside it, which Roper used when his black cab arrived.

Joe Baxter and Sam Hall were on the entrance in black tie, controlling the line. They came down and helped Roper out of his cab.

'Great to see you, Major,' Joe said, and pushed him up the ramp.

There was a young punk in a silk bomber jacket standing with two girls at the front of the line. 'You've got to be a bloody cripple to get service here.'

Sam Hall, almost casually, slapped him back-handed across the face, then grabbed him by the front of the jacket. 'That man is probably the biggest hero you ever set eyes on, sunshine. So you get to go to the back of the line. Alternatively, you could just sod off.'

The youth put his hands up. 'Okay.' Then he pulled the girls away and went.

Joe Baxter said, 'Sorry about that, Major.'

'Sticks and stones, Joe, I couldn't care less. I'm lucky to be here.'

They went inside and the head waiter, a dark, energetic Portuguese named Fernando, came forward. 'Major Roper, a pleasure. I'll lead the way.'

With Baxter at the helm, they followed Fernando into the restaurant, which was beautifully designed in Art Deco. There was a small dance floor, a four-piece band and cocktail bar straight out of the thirties. The waiters wore cruise-ship monkey jackets. The Salters, Ferguson and his people were all in the largest booth. Harry got up and ruffled Roper's shoulder-length hair.

'You still go round like a bloody hippie.'

'I express my individuality, Harry.'

Salter looked down into that burned, ravaged face and gave him a hug. 'You're a real piece of work, Roper.'

'Now don't take pity on me, Harry. If that gets out in the East End, you'll be finished.' He turned to Ferguson. 'Okay. Most of this you know, some you don't. The whole thing with Holstein Heath, of course, is that due to an error, it was never East German or West. If anything, it was neo-Nazi, even though von Berger never belonged to the party. He's kept the flame alight. For years after the war, all the police there were former SS, and so on.'

He took a drink of whiskey. 'Von Berger frequently visits Schloss Adler, often with Rossi. They come in by helicopter at a landing area close to the Schloss, but it's a huge meadow and they can actually land a plane on it, too.'

'Do we have any kind of connection there?' Ferguson asked.

'It's a tight-knit community. As a matter of interest, though, about forty kilometres from Neustadt, on the edge of the *Schwarze Platz*, is a small village called Arnheim. There's a handful of houses, but also an old Luftwaffe base from the Second World War. It's dilapidated, but it has a landing strip that can take most things, and it's used by a man called Max Kubel.' He turned to Ferguson. 'He's been on your list out there for a number of years. A smuggler of most things, including people to the West, flies an old Storch plane on special jobs. His father was Luftwaffe in the war. He knows Neustadt very well. I've spoken to him.'

'Yes, well, knowing is one thing and being able to access the place is something else,' Dillon said.

'He does a lot of cigarette-smuggling, uses people. He has one guy named Hans Klein in Neustadt, who was forced off his farm by the Baron and hates him. He could be a useful source of information.'

At that moment, Fernando appeared and said to Salter, 'I'm so sorry. A Baron von Berger and a Signor Rossi are at the entrance to see you?'

Salter looked at Ferguson, and Ferguson nodded. Fernando went off, and Ferguson said, 'Everyone, just go with the flow.'

The Baron came down the steps, followed by Rossi and Derry Gibson. 'Why, what a surprise, General,' he said to Ferguson.

'I doubt it,' Ferguson said.

Dillon grinned up at Gibson. 'Derry, you were lucky not to get wet.'

Gibson smiled reluctantly. 'Damn you, Sean.'

'Oh, that's already taken care of.'

Salter said, 'Would you like a table, Baron? I think we can manage that.'

'Thank you, but Art Deco has never appealed. I just wanted to say hello.' He smiled. 'And that I'm thinking of you all.' He turned to Rossi and Gibson. 'We can go.' He looked back at Ferguson and Dillon. 'Take care now. I wouldn't want anything to happen to you.'

They walked out. Harry said, 'I don't know what that was all about.' He shook his head at Dillon. 'Let the old bastard do his worst.'

'That was the point, Harry. He's daring us to do *our* worst.'

Outside, the three of them drove away, and Rossi leaned forward and closed the divider.

The Baron said, 'So you've made a decision?'

'Yes. It's Ferguson first. I'm going to kidnap him.'

'I love it,' Gibson said.

'What's the point of that?' the Baron asked Marco.

'I'm going to take him to Schloss Adler and . . . explore the market, shall we say. With all Ferguson's experience, I'm sure, everyone would love to have a piece of him. The Russians, the Arabs, you name it.'

'Come on, Marco, you can't fool me. The only reason you want to get your hands on Ferguson in this way would be to pull in Dillon – because you know very well that Dillon would come to his rescue.'

Marco smiled happily. 'Let him try.'

'I think you underestimate Dillon, Marco. You've underestimated him from the beginning. Never play with a tiger. Finish him off – before he turns on you. But it's your play. If you want to do this, I won't give you my blessing, but I won't stand in your way.'

'Thank you, father.'

'Give me a cigarette.' Rossi did, and the Baron sat back to smoke it, thinking of his son, his handsome son, Yale University, the war hero with the medals, and yet, in the end, so stupid.

178

GERMANY
LONDON
GERMANY

13

Max Kubel had been sitting in a bar in Berlin, the Tabu, when he had taken Roper's call on his mobile. Born in 1957, he was the only son of one of the great Luftwaffe night fighter aces of the Second World War, also named Max Kubel, and a Knight's Cross holder. He'd been another example of a man who couldn't let go after the war, and had made a living out of flying in and out of East Germany in the Cold War days, once too often, as it happened, when a Russian MiG fighter downed him one night in 1973.

Because of his father's record, Max had been allowed into a government-sponsored scheme to train as a pilot with the German Luftwaffe. That was both good and bad. He had a flair for it, like his father, but a restless temperament not much suited to discipline.

The years had rolled by, rather boringly, the German government's reluctance to commit to combat situations leaving little room for his father's kind of war, and Max had worshipped his father's exploits, his life. In his case, there was no combat, just flying into countries in Africa or the Middle East on behalf of the United Nations, cargo planes, humanitarian work, and he hated it.

And then, out of Saudi and skirting Iraq, flying three UN peace officials, he'd been bounced by an Iraqi MiG and fired on. He had pulled his father's old Luftwaffe trick, gone down low and used full flaps at the last moment, and the MiG had gone headfirst into the desert to avoid him. The three UN officials had been delighted at still being in the land of the living. One of them, an Irish woman, had said he deserved a medal. Instead, the Luftwaffe had thrown him out for flouting their no-combat rules.

Since then, he'd discovered the lucrative delights of various kinds of smuggling using an old Storch from the Second World War, doing night runs, sometimes as far as Poland.

He had fair hair and insolent blue eyes and wore his father's old black leather Luftwaffe flying jacket, his personal talisman, and he sat there, thinking about the phone call. Roper had been impressive, had even managed fluent German. The mention of Ferguson was enough. Roper had said he only wanted information on the Baron's movements at Neustadt, but there had to be more to it than that. It was quite exciting, really. He was aware of the Baron's background, knew of the whispers about who Rossi was, had a professional's respect for his flying record. No, the prospect intrigued, and he did have that drunken oaf, Hans Klein, to call on, who helped him occasionally on cigarette runs. A bar girl approached him, he waved her away and dialled Klein's number. After a while there was an answer.

The words were slurred. He'd been drinking. 'Who is this?'

'Max Kubel. Where are you living now?'

'Not much better than a pigsty. The cottage at the back of the church. You know the Baron robbed me of my farm, and that son of his . . .'

'Beat the shit out of you.'

'I'll have my day. What do you want? Are you doing another run?'

'Soon, Hans, but I need to know what's going on in Neustadt. The Baron's movements, and Rossi's. Are they in or out?'

'Why?'

'Because I'll pay you well, you stupid bastard, and you'll do it anyway because you hate them. You've got my mobile number, so get on with it.'

He switched off, feeling suddenly incredibly cheerful, and the bar girl came back and stroked his hair. 'A drink, Max?'

He ran a hand up her leg. 'Very definitely. Whisky, *liebling*, malt whisky. We'll both have one.'

'And then? Can I come back?'

'We'll see, Elsa, we'll see.'

At Harry's Place, they reached the end of their meal and split up. On the pavement, as they all started for their cars, Dillon said, 'I'll hang on with Roper and share his cab.'

'If you like,' Ferguson said.

They departed, the cab drove up, the driver got out and put the ramp down and Dillon pushed Roper inside. 'Stable Mews,' he called to the driver when he got in, and turned to Roper. 'On your way.'

'What are you up to?'

'Me? Nothing. I'm restless, that's all.'

'That's when I worry about you.'

'No need.'

'I don't believe that for a moment.'

'He murdered Sara Hesser.' Dillon lit a cigarette. 'I've never been so certain of anything in my life. I should shoot him, but Ferguson says no, even though we've taken out people as bad as Rossi before.'

'Maybe Ferguson is intent on handling this differently.'

'And maybe Marco Rossi has his own ideas about handling. Maybe he's a lot like me.' The cab drew up in Stable Mews and Dillon got out.

Roper said, 'Sean – whatever it is – don't.'

'You're a great guy, Roper, one of the few people in this rotten old world I truly admire, but, as we say in Belfast, goodnight to you.'

He let himself into the cottage, went upstairs, changed into jeans and a bomber jacket, went down, opened the secret drawer under the stairs, selected a Walther and slipped it into the back of his jeans. He left a few moments later in his Mini Cooper.

After the meeting at Harry's Place, Rossi had phoned Newton and Cook and told them to report to South Audley Street.

'You stay on Ferguson. First thing tomorrow, you find out every single place he goes.'

'But why?' Newton said. 'What's the purpose of this?'

'The purpose, you stupid oaf, is that we're going to lift him at the right moment.'

There was consternation on both faces. 'Now look here,' Cook said. 'We're not into that.'

Marco Rossi said, 'You're into what I say you are or I'll see you never work again. Do what you're told and don't fuck with me.'

There was a moment of hesitation, then Newton said, 'As you say, Mr Rossi.'

'Right, get on with it. And don't use your car. Get a white van, something anonymous, right?'

They went out and Gibson, who'd been in the room, watching, said, 'They used to be SAS? No wonder the Provos did so well. What happens now?'

'There's an old airbase at Fotley; it's got a decaying runway but it's usable. I'll have one of our planes left there. When we lift Ferguson, I'll fly it myself.'

'To where?'

'Schloss Adler. The game starts there. The game, Derry, that will bring in Sean Dillon.'

'Well, that will suit me fine.'

In South Audley Street, Dillon left the Mini and walked through light rain to the side street where the Rashid house stood. He stood in the shadows and watched, and suddenly the door opened and Newton and Cook emerged. He recognized them at once and drew back into the shadows. They crossed to their car and got in. It was only then that Dillon hurried across the street, opened the door and put the muzzle of his Walther to Newton's temple.

'Hello, guys, am I your worst nightmare or not?'

Newton said, 'Christ, it's you, Dillon.'

'As ever was. What's going on with Rossi?'

'For God's sake, we just work for Rashid on security. He's our new boss. That's all, I swear.'

He was genuinely fearful and Dillon sensed it. 'Okay, piss off, but come up against me and I'll kill you, both of you.'

They drove away. Dillon turned to walk and the door opened and Rossi emerged in a blue tracksuit, a towel at his throat. He started to run.

Dillon called, 'Hey, you bastard.'

Rossi paused, turned and saw him. 'Dillon, is that you? What are you going to do, shoot me?'

'I'd love to, but you've been put off limits for the moment.' Dillon shook out a cigarette and lit it. 'Killing the old woman – a big war hero like you. It couldn't have given you much of a kick.'

'Fuck you, Dillon,' Rossi said.

'You've got it wrong. Right time, right place, I'll kill you, Marco. She was a nice old lady. You shouldn't have done it.'

He turned and walked away. Marco Rossi took a deep breath and started to run again. Behind him, the front door of the house gently closed. The Baron had followed him, had wanted a word, and instead, had heard everything. He turned, and with a heavy heart mounted the stairs.

The Daimler picked Ferguson up the following morning at Cavendish Place, where Newton and Cook were parked in a British Telecom van, wearing appropriate yellow anoraks. They followed at a discreet distance to Harley Street, watched the Daimler park and waited, Cook opening the rear door of the van, taking out a large tool box and looking busy. Newton strolled up the street, glancing at the brass nameplate on the door as he passed, and returned to Cook.

He leaned against the van and lit a cigarette. 'Some surgeon, name of Merriman.'

Professor Henry Merriman was a large, avuncular man who greeted Ferguson warmly. A young nurse stood at a side table, various medical items laid out beside her.

'A pleasure, General. We'll get straight on with it. It's a very quick procedure. Just strip to the waist and Emily here will take care of your things.' He went to the table.

Ferguson took off his jacket, tie and shirt. 'I hope it doesn't hurt,' he said cheerfully.

'Nothing a little local anaesthetic can't handle.' He turned, a small plastic ampoule in his hand. 'Sit down, please, and raise your left arm. It's instant.'

A slight prick and his skin was numb. 'Excellent,' Ferguson said.

Emily was standing with what looked like a small aluminium pistol in one hand. Merriman took it from her. 'I call it my stun gun, but that's a joke.' He placed the muzzle against Ferguson's armpit, pulled a trigger. There was the slightest of clicks. He smiled. 'You can get dressed.'

He handed the gun to the girl. Ferguson picked up his shirt. 'That's it? What happens now?'

'Nothing. Your implant is already code-indexed into the Omega programme's computer. Where you go, it goes – any corner of the world.'

Ferguson finished dressing. It made him feel rather gloomy. 'What about the toilet? Will it locate me there?'

The young nurse found this very funny and laughed. Merriman smiled. 'A possibility.'

Ferguson said, 'Good morning, Professor. It's been a sincere treat.'

Dillon called in at Roper's and found him, as usual, at the computer banks. He paused from what he was doing. 'Did you do something stupid?'

'I suppose so.' Dillon told him what had happened.

'Damn you, Sean, for an idiot. You're baiting; stirring the pot.'

'It's Rossi. I want to see him in . . .'

'I know – hell. Have you told Ferguson?'

'No. He wouldn't be pleased. Anyway, he was doing the Omega thing today. Can you access that?'

'I can access anything, Dillon. I've already extracted his index code.'

'But he only had it this morning.'

'The microchip is precoded into the system, so he's on the system from the moment he's implanted. Watch.' His fingers danced over the keys. A map of England appeared. 'There he is, the yellow luminous dot. Now we go in closer – London, and there's the dot again. Closer, and there we are. Pall Mall and moving. Knowing Ferguson, I'd say lunch at the Reform Club.'

'Thanks for the information, but I'll keep out of his way,' and Dillon left.

Rossi landed at Fotley, the old RAF airbase he had chosen, and found Gibson waiting for him. Rossi taxied to the end of the runway and turned, then switched off and got out and Gibson drove up to him.

'You found it, then?' Rossi said.

'I must have done; I'm here, aren't I? Queer sort of place. Everything looks as if it's falling down.'

'It is, the war was a long time ago, but the runway's still sound and that's all that matters.'

'Twenty miles, I made it.'

'That's what I figured. Back to town.'

'To what?' Derry asked, as he turned onto a country road.

'You'll see.'

To his astonishment, what he returned to was not what he had expected. The Rolls was parked outside the Rashid house, the chauffeur loading luggage into the boot. The Baron appeared out of the door in his trilby and black leather coat and leaning on his cane.

Rossi said to Gibson, 'Pull over and leave this to me.' He approached von Berger. 'Father, what is this?'

'I've decided to go away, Marco. To Schloss Adler.'

'But why?'

'I need time to think. I heard you and Dillon last night, my son. You lied to me. You shouldn't have done it. It wasn't honourable.'

'But, father . . .'

The Baron said nothing more. He got in the Rolls, the chauffeur slipped behind the wheel, and they drove away. Gibson said, 'What in the hell was that all about?'

'Dillon,' Rossi said. 'Damn him. He's been a stone in my shoe too long. I'll have him.' At that moment, his mobile sounded, and when he answered, Newton said. 'We're around the corner from the Reform Club in Pall Mall. Ferguson's gone in.'

'Probably for lunch,' Rossi said. 'Okay, don't stay. Go to Cavendish Place and set up there. I'll send Gibson to join you. We're going to do it today.'

'Now look,' Newton said, 'I'm not sure about this . . .'

'I am. Listen to me, Newton. I can finish you. Or I can give you a nice fat fee. Which is it? In or out?'

Greed, and fear, of course, won the day. 'In.'

Dillon turned up at the Ministry of Defence, and found Hannah in the main office at her computer. She stopped and leaned back to look at him.

'What's up?'

'Why should anything be up?'

'I know my Sean.'

'Oh, I suppose I was a bit stupid last night.'

'Tell me.'

Which he did, lighting a cigarette and looking out of the window. When he finished, she said, 'You fool.'

'I know. It's Rossi and what he did. I can't get Sara Hesser out of my mind.'

'Sean, I've a psychology degree, so here's a free reading. Oh, Rossi did the murder, but you feel as guilty as hell because you gave that woman a promise. What was it? "No harm will come to you on this earth, I swear it"?'

Dillon, never so emotional in his life, said, 'And remember what happened? She touched my face and said, "I believe you. You're a good man in spite of yourself."' She had never seen him so haggard and drawn.

'Me, the great Sean Dillon, and you know what happened and who was responsible, and I'll see Rossi in hell for it.'

He turned and found the door to Ferguson's office open, and the general standing in the doorway. 'Then you'll go straight down the same road to hell yourself, Dillon. What on earth did you think you were doing? Confrontation, direct threats? It's not the way to handle things at the moment. You were totally out of order.'

'I usually am.'

'Right, you're suspended. Leave the office now. I'll speak to you again at what I consider to be an appropriate time. You will surrender all your weapons.'

Dillon managed a gentle smile. 'Ah, well, Charles, I always thought the day would come, but you've been a decent ould stick, and in spite of Serbia in the old days, when you sold me out, you've treated me well.' He turned to Hannah.

'Oh, Sean,' she said.

'I know. I always take the hard approach and I know that doesn't hold with your fine Jewish morality, but revenge is a concept not unknown in the Old Testament. I'll be on my way, and God bless all here.'

He disappeared and Ferguson said, 'Damn him. Why did he do it? It unscrambles things in the wrong way.'

'It's simple, sir. He can be more emotional than you think. He's put himself on the line for me in the past, for you. All he could think of was an old lady who trusted him and ended up in the river. In spite of everything Dillon's done, if you want a psychopath here, it's not him, it's Marco Rossi.'

'To hell with it, I'm going home. Order the Daimler.'

'It's not available, General. Out for maintenance today, remember?'

'Then get me a bloody taxi,' and he stormed back into his office.

Dillon sat in his Mini Cooper, thinking about things. Well, everything had to come to an end, that was life. Still and all, there'd been a lot of water under the bridge. He reached for a cigarette, lit it, looked out and saw Ferguson walk to a waiting black taxi and get in. It moved off, and Dillon started up the Mini Cooper and went after him. There was no logical reason that he should, except perhaps for some instinct, an Irish thing; but he did, eased out into the traffic and followed the cab.

In Cavendish Place, Newton and Cook had taken up a manhole to explain their presence. Derry Gibson, also wearing a yellow Telecom jacket, sat inside the van reading a newspaper. Newton moved to the passenger window.

'Come on, it's been nearly four hours. Are we getting anywhere?'

At that moment, a black cab drew up. Derry said, 'I think we might be,' and then Ferguson got out and paid the driver, who drove away.

'Now,' Gibson said and opened the small leather case on the seat beside him and took out a small plastic ampoule. 'Get him.'

He got out, and as Ferguson turned away, they grabbed him by each arm and Gibson moved in. 'A real pleasure, General,' and he jabbed Ferguson in the neck. The effect was almost instantaneous. Ferguson sagged, they walked him to the back of the van, Gibson opened the door and they put him inside, Gibson following. 'Get going,' he said.

Dillon, turning in at the entrance to Cavendish Place, saw everything and put his foot down. A delivery van drove in front of him. Dillon braked and swerved. Beyond him, the Telecom van swung out into the traffic. He joined in, well behind. The heavy London traffic made things difficult, but he managed to stay focused on the Telecom van.

He got out his Codex Four and checked into Hannah, who answered at once. 'I followed Ferguson home. He was jumped by Derry Gibson, Newton and Cook, and dumped in a fake British Telecom van. I'm following.'

'Where, for God's sake?'

'North London. I don't know. Essex way. Get in touch with Roper. He can invoke the Omega thing. That should tell you where we're going. Tell him to keep me informed.'

Derry Gibson called Marco Rossi. 'We've bagged the bird.'

'I'm on my way. I'll see you at Fotley.'

'Well, let's hope you're there before we are. Kidnapping draws at least ten years in this country.'

* * *

Roper cut into Dillon. 'I've heard the story, I'm on the case. Omega is working fine. I'll track and keep you informed. No reason to worry if you lose him. I'll put you back on track.'

Dillon had a thought. 'These three goons are working for Rossi, so where are they going?'

'Maybe it's where are they flying? I'll check.'

As he emerged from London, the traffic thinned a little, not all that much, but enough to keep Dillon well back. Roper came on.

'The Baron just left Northolt, destination Munich. I've checked there. He's got a helicopter booked for Neustadt.'

'Has he now?'

'Even more interesting: Rossi had a plane delivered to a place called Fotley in Essex this morning. It's an old RAF airbase, now disused, with a long runway. I think that's where you're going. I hope you make it, Sean. Are you carrying?'

'I damn well am. But what if I fail? Where are they going?'

'Well, Omega will confirm, but I think we both know. Schloss Adler.'

'Right, then I suggest you get on to this Max Kubel. He can alert the Klein man at Neustadt. Tell Kubel to put in place whatever plan we'd need to mount a rescue operation. It'll be a huge payday for him. I'll press on and hope to catch them at Fotley.'

In the end, he failed, mainly because of a farm tractor on a narrow country road. He finally made the old airfield only to see the abandoned van and the Gulfstream already moving. As it lifted and roared past, Newton looked out.

'Jesus,' he said. 'That's Dillon's Mini Cooper.'

'Is that a fact?' Derry Gibson laughed. Ferguson, unconscious, was strapped in one of the seats. Derry patted his cheek. 'I'll go and tell Rossi. He'll be so pleased.'

At Arnheim, Max Kubel was working on the Storch prior to a foray into Poland. He'd always remembered the adage

192

from the Second World War: half the airmen who die aren't shot down by the enemy. They die of engine failure. It was why he'd always taken care of his own maintenance. He closed the engine cowling and slapped the fuselage, which had a fresh coat of dull black paint.

'Good girl,' he said, and his mobile went.

He listened to Roper for a long five minutes and was immediately interested and full of energy. 'I'll talk to Klein.'

'This meadow outside the Schloss, can it accommodate Rossi's plane, especially at night?'

'It's huge, and the Schloss is floodlit. There's plenty of light.'

'So what would we do? Could you fly in while Dillon attempts a recovery?'

'Come off it. The minute I attempted a landing, the whole thing would be blown.'

'Then how would we get to Neustadt? What could we do? Parachute in? Dillon's done that before.'

'Not into Schloss Adler. Battlements, courtyards, roofs – it isn't nice.'

'Then when you want to make a nefarious trip into Holstein Heath, how do you do it? I know how mysterious the damn place is. The locals must be suspicious of any kind of strangers.'

'Yes, but if I put a group together for an in-and-out job, they won't look like strangers. The police in Holstein Heath look very like the Vopos of the old East German days. Believe it or not, they still use Russian Cossack motorcycles and field cars.'

'So what are you saying?'

'In the past, I've gone in with my people when I've needed them, using those vehicles and uniforms. Would Dillon buy that?'

'Well, his German is fluent.'

'He couldn't do it on his own.'

'What about you?'

'No way. My task would be to do the extracting. Dillon and whoever, helped by Klein's intelligence, pull Ferguson, and all hell breaks out, so the smart thing would be for me to fly in from Arnheim. It's a short flight, I'd drop in at the Schloss in my Storch and pick them up.'

'And you're confident you could do that?'

'To the great Kubel, anything is possible, and to avoid any problem with angry foresters, it would be the only way. These are the Baron's people.'

'You mean it's Indian territory?'

'Exactly. Another thing. In the Storch, I could manage Ferguson, but only two others. Two men only to take on the situation at the castle. I've got an idea that Dillon's that crazy, but does he know someone else who is?'

'Oh, yes,' Roper said. 'I think so. There's a big payday for you on this, by the way.'

'Stuff the payday, I've been getting stale and I've looked you up, Roper. You're what the Jews call a *mensch*. I'm a great admirer.'

'Flattery is always appreciated.'

'I'll speak to Klein and get things moving.'

At his cottage behind the church at Neustadt, Klein took the call from Kubel and listened to what he had to say.

'So what do you want me to do?'

'Let me know the minute the Baron turns up in the helicopter. After that, Rossi in his plane. Can you get into the Schloss?'

'Of course I can. I've known it backwards since I was a child.'

'In spite of security?'

'The security is crap. I can go around all that.'

'Get this right, Hans. There's a lot of money in it for you.'

'And where the Baron is concerned, it will be a pleasure. I'll go and check things out up there.'

Kubel switched off and Klein pulled on a hunting jacket, put a sawn-off shotgun in one pocket, a double handful of cartridges in the other and went out, smiling.

On the final stretch back to London, Dillon listened to everything Roper had to say. 'Fine,' he said. 'Alert Hannah. Tell her to book Lacey and Parry. Alert the quartermaster. The destination will be Arnheim.'

'There's one thing, Sean,' Roper said. 'You can't do this on your own. Don't tell me you're going to ride a Cossack through the *Schwarze Platz* and do a "Dirty Harry". You need a friend.'

'I'll get a friend.'

'You're sure?'

'Trust me. I'll ask him, and for this, he'll be there.'

Dillon turned down to Hangman's Wharf and the Dark Man, parked and went inside. There were only a couple of customers, Dora at the bar, and Harry and Billy in their usual corner booth. Harry looked up and frowned.

'You look stressed.'

'You could say that.' Dillon sat down. 'Just listen.'

When he was finished, Harry said, 'I knew that Rossi was bad news.'

Dillon's phone sounded and Roper said, 'No question, Sean, it's Neustadt they're aiming for. Everything all right with you? The extra man?'

'We'll see.'

'I'm sure you will.' He switched off.

Dillon said, 'Billy. You heard the story. I'm going to go in like a Vopo on a Cossack. It's a good thing I speak German.'

'Which I don't, but you need a gun, and I can wear one of these Vopo uniforms as well as you can.' Billy had that cold, pale smile on his face.

It was Harry who cut in. 'We'd better get sorted, Dillon. We can't leave Ferguson in the hands of these bastards. Anyway, I like the old sod. You and Billy do it. Billy's come on a bit since you took him in hand. Right, Billy? Likes doing something because it's the right thing to do.'

'I should say so.' Billy got up. 'I'll go and pack.' He smiled to Dillon. 'This is getting to be a habit.'

At Farley Field, Dillon arrived to surprises. First of all, the presence of Hannah Bernstein. He said, 'What in the hell are you doing here?'

'I speak German, Sean, and it's my boss at the sharp end. I think I should be here.'

Then the Salter Rolls appeared, and disgorged not only Billy but Harry, both with hand luggage.

Dillon said, 'What is this?'

'This German police thing. I'm going with you. I'll stay back at base with the Superintendent, if you want, but you always want to do it on your own. Well, this time, you can't. It's too important.'

Dillon said, 'Fine, just don't get in the way.' He walked towards the Citation, and Lacey came out, dressed in anonymous flying overalls. 'You know what we're up to here?'

'The superintendent filled us in. You'll notice we've sprayed over our RAF roundels. Don't want anybody identifying us.'

'You know where we're going?'

'Roper's told us. Sean, this is something else. I mean, the general.'

'Don't worry, I'll bring him back, I swear it. I don't want crew, just you and Parry. Board and I'll see the quartermaster with Billy.'

The department's quartermaster waited with his list.

'All loaded, Mr Dillon. Walthers and Carswell silencers, three MP40 machine pistols.'

'That's going back a bit.'

'I've checked, Mr Dillon, and the police in Holstein Heath area are rather old-fashioned. I would point out that the Schmeisser is still an extremely efficient weapon. Some stun grenades. Some smoke. That should do you in the present circumstances.'

'You know what they are?'

'Mr Dillon,' the sergeant major said. 'Twenty-five years ago in the Grenadier Guards, I was trying to hunt you down in the IRA in South Armagh, and failed. I'm glad, because it means you're here to save the general, who is one of the finest men I've ever known. Now, I'll load these items for you, sir, and you'll return them to me when you get back.'

Dillon walked out with Billy, who said, 'Well, he's got faith in you.'

'A lot of people do. It can be a burden, Billy. Come on, let's go. We're not saving the world, this time, we're saving Charles Ferguson.'

He went up the Airstair door, followed by Billy. Parry closed the door as they joined Harry and Hannah. A few moments later, the engines turned over on the Citation and it lifted up into the sky.

14

Charles Ferguson came back to the real world to find himself on a bed in a dark, panelled bedroom. The door was locked, and when he went to the window, the fall was at least a hundred feet. It was immediately apparent that there was nowhere he could go. He was standing at the window, looking out, when the door opened. Derry Gibson came in.

'Ah, there you are, General. You look well.'

'Well, I've felt better. Where's Rossi?'

'Busy elsewhere. You'll have to compose yourself, the grand man you are. I'll see you get some food.'

The door closed, and Ferguson looked out of the window again, suddenly more alone than he'd ever felt. 'God dammit,' he thought. 'You were right, Dillon.'

At the same time, Rossi found his father in the Great Hall. The Baron was sitting by the fire, a drink at his hand.

Marco said, 'Father, I think we should talk.'

'I think we should, too. Have you succeeded in your endeavour?'

'If you mean have I lifted Ferguson, yes. He's here in the Schloss.'

'And you intend your purpose?'

'I don't see why not.'

'And Dillon?'

'Hot on the trail.'

'And that's what you want? A face-to-face confrontation?'

'Any time he likes.'

The Baron nodded. 'I've given things a great deal of thought. I just don't know if I agree.'

'It's in motion, Father. Everything. I must see it through.'

'Must you? Unless I am mistaken, this is still Schloss Adler. I am still the Baron. Let me think about this, Marco. Me, your father.' And at that moment, the young SS *Sturmbannführer* was in charge again. 'I'll let you know what I want. What *I* want, not you. Now, please, go away for the moment.'

Hans Klein had gone in at the lowest end of the Schloss, and found what he called the chamber entrance, a great grille overgrown by shrubbery. It was a legacy of German army engineering, when the Schloss had been used as a command headquarters and the whole drainage system had been modernized.

Klein lifted the grille, moved in and switched on his light. The concrete tunnel was dry, except for a steady stream of water down a centre channel. Klein walked along one of the sides, reached a steel ladder and climbed up, raising the manhole cover at the top.

He emerged into a basement area that he knew well, filled with storage rooms and kitchen areas, gradually reaching up to the glories of the Great Hall. He often penetrated that far, when the Baron and Rossi were away. It always gave him a feeling of power.

Now, as he hovered in the basement area, he became aware of voices resonating and quickly withdrew and went back down the ladder. When he emerged into the wooded area, he replaced the grille, moved away, squatted down by a tree and called Kubel.

Afterwards, Kubel spoke to Roper. 'All systems go. His secret way into the Schloss works. When the Gulfstream landed, he saw Rossi, and four other men, one of them being supported between two others.'

'The general. Probably Newton and Cook holding him up, plus Derry Gibson.'

'That would make sense.'

'Are you going to be ready for us, Max? The right gear?'

'All here, so I won't need help, which means security will be nice and tight. We'll be ready, Roper, whenever your friends are.'

It was a couple of hours later that a key rattled in the door. Ferguson turned and Rossi came in, with Derry Gibson.

'I just wanted to make sure you were comfortable.'

'How kind. When do I get to see the Baron?'

'When he wants to see you. Compose yourself; your turn will come.'

He turned away. Ferguson said, 'You seem to be going to a lot of trouble. I'd have thought you'd have given me a bullet in the head by now.'

Rossi smiled. 'Not for you, General; you're much too valuable.'

'What happens to me then?'

'I'll probably sell you to the Arabs,' Rossi said, and the door closed.

At the same moment at Arnheim, they all grouped around the table in Max Kubel's office and examined the map.

'That's it,' Kubel said. 'Neustadt.' He turned to Dillon. 'It's an old-fashioned motorcycle, the Cossack.'

'Don't worry, I'll manage,' Dillon said. He turned to Billy. 'You get the sidecar.'

Kubel said, 'Thanks to these mobiles you've brought, we'll be in constant touch. You should get there in an hour at the most. Once you bring him out, I can make the meadow in twenty minutes. I'll be sitting in the cockpit, ready to go.'

'That sounds reasonable,' Dillon said. 'How about you, Billy?'

'I'm always reasonable.'

'Once you leave, I'll call Klein. He'll be waiting. His place is the only cottage at the back of the church. You can't miss it.' He glanced around the table. 'How does it sound?'

Lacey and Parry looked dubious. It was Hannah who said, 'The whole thing seems to depend on split-second timing.'

'Absolutely, but it is possible. The distances involved are not great.'

'Well, in the circumstances,' Harry Salter said, 'can they get on with it? It's not good for my nerves.'

'Exactly,' Billy said. 'Personally, I can't wait to dress as a copper. The old lags I was with at Wandsworth will never believe it.'

'Fine, this way then,' Kubel said.

In the hangar, the Storch waited, black, like something from another time. The old Cossack motorcycle waited, too. Everyone waited, uncertainty thick in the air. Kubel stood with Lacey and Parry, and looked out as it started to rain.

'Not good,' Lacey said.

'It never is when good is needed, Squadron Leader, haven't you noticed that?'

A door clanged, they turned, and Dillon and Billy emerged, strange and menacing figures from the past in their steel helmets, Vopo uniforms and despatch riders' raincoats. Each had a Schmeisser machine pistol slung across the chest. Dillon was fastening his helmet strap.

'Have you got everything?' Kubel asked.

'Absolutely. Big pockets. Extra magazines, a Walther apiece, stick grenade in the boot. Just like the old days.'

'Christ, you look like you're going to make a D-Day movie,' Salter said.

'Who knows?' Dillon looked out. 'Nice evening for it.' He turned. 'You up for this, Billy?'

'Let's get going, for God's sake. We're going to get bleeding soaked.'

He settled himself in the sidecar, and Dillon mounted the Cossack and kicked it into life. Hannah ran forward and put a hand on his sleeve.

'Sean?' Her face was desperate.

'We'll bring him back.' He smiled. 'You worry too much,' and he drove away into the driving rain.

The road into the *Schwarze Platz* was well surfaced, but quite narrow, the forest crowding in, and already the gloom of early evening was turning towards darkness. The rain was relentless, and both Dillon and Billy wore goggles. The Cossack responded well and there was little traffic. Twice, they passed farm trucks going in the other direction, and once a sedan.

Dillon turned and shouted to Billy, 'We'll be there sooner than Kubel thought,' and in spite of the weather, he pushed the Cossack up to sixty.

At the Schloss, the Baron sat by the log fire as Rossi came in with Ferguson. Newton and Cook stood on either side of the grand stairway on the landing, holding AK47s. Derry Gibson stood to one side of the fireplace.

'Ah, there you are, General. Join me. Perhaps you'd like a drink?'

'How very kind. A large whisky would do it.'

'Marco.'

It was an order and Rossi went to a sideboard, poured the whisky, and Ferguson savoured it. 'Your chaps look as if they're expecting trouble.'

'No, actually we're expecting Dillon,' Rossi said.

'How on earth would he know where I was?' Ferguson was wary. Could they know about Omega?

'Because he saw you being kidnapped and chased us all the way to Fotley airfield. Arrived just too late.'

'How unfortunate.'

'It certainly was for you.'

The Baron said, 'Enough, Marco. Let's show our guest some courtesy.' He got up and leaned on his cane. 'Come with me, General, and I'll show you some of the rarer sights of the Schloss.' He led the way to a door beside the stairway and nodded to Marco, who opened it. 'A tunnel built in the fifteenth century to give access to the chapel, which incidentally is very fine. Let's take a look,' and he led the way in.

At that moment, Dillon was kicking on Klein's door. After a while, it opened and Klein stood there. He recoiled instinctively at the uniforms. They pushed him back inside.

'Don't worry, we're from Kubel,' Dillon said in German. 'Are you ready to take us in?'

'Yes,' Klein said eagerly. He reeked of drink, but turned, took down his hunting coat and put the sawn-off shotgun in one of the pockets.

Dillon called Kubel on his Codex Four. It was answered instantly. 'We're here already and we've made contact with Klein, so we're going straight in. To hell with waiting. You said it would take you twenty minutes. Leave in fifteen.'

'I'm your man,' Kubel said. 'Good luck.'

Dillon said to Billy, 'Right, let's get it done.' He turned to Klein. 'My friend doesn't speak German. Just lead the way and let's get on with it.'

The Baron leading, they went into the chapel, the candles guttering, the great bowl of the eternal flame burning. The heraldic banners hung from each side of the roof in the gloom.

'Seven hundred years of my family's history, General.'

'Very impressive,' Ferguson said. 'No hint of the Third Reich. I see no Nazi banners.'

'But I was never a member of the Nazi Party.'

'However, you did give distinguished service to the SS.'

'The Waffen SS, the greatest fighting soldiers the world has ever seen.'

'That's one point of view. And you were Hitler's aide.'

'True, but he had many. I was an office boy, if you like.'

'Come now, entrusted with the holiest of missions?'

'On the whim of a man who had become unbalanced at the end. Wait there.'

He walked behind the mausoleum, opened the secret cavity, took out the diary and held it up. 'You think this is what it's all about, the Führer's diary, a "holy book"?'

'That's what Sara Hesser told me.'

'Wrong. My family motto is: "A Matter of Honour". The Führer's mission got me out of Berlin, gave me money to make a fresh start. Because of that, it is a matter of honour to guard it. Oh, some of the information, particularly that affecting the President, could be useful, but that was never the point of my feud with you.'

He replaced the diary, Ferguson heard a creak as the cavity closed. 'So what is the point?'

'Kate Rashid saved my life in Baghdad. Dillon killed her brothers and was responsible for her death – and through him, you.'

'So I'm to pay the blood price?'

'Dillon will also pay if, as my son hopes, he comes for you.'

'So what's my price?'

'We'll go back to the hall and discuss it.'

In spite of the floodlighting of the Schloss, the wooded area on the slopes was dark and gloomy, as Klein led the way through the shrubbery to the chamber entrance and removed the grille. He went down the steps, switched on a large flashlight and splayed it across the concrete tunnel.

'Here we are. Takes us straight into the heart of the Schloss.' He took out half a bottle of schnapps and poured it down.

'Good,' Dillon said. 'But cut that out. We need you sober.'

At the same moment at Arnheim, Max Kubel boosted power and let the Storch go, the Argus engine responding magnificently. He lifted off into the rain.

The others stood watching. Hannah said, 'It's all up to Dillon now.'

'Well, it usually bleeding is,' Harry Salter said.

When they emerged into the basement area, Klein led the way through a series of deserted corridors and kitchens. 'No servants?' Dillon asked.

'I checked in the village. He only keeps a handful. He's given them all time off.'

They went up a flight of stairs, and he opened a door cautiously. 'The Outer Hall,' he whispered. It was dark. They could hear voices close by. 'They must be in the Great Hall,' Klein said. 'Follow me. If we go up the stairway over there, there's a place where you can look down.'

He swallowed more schnapps while Dillon explained to Billy, and they moved on, their weapons at the ready.

15

Seated by the fire again, Ferguson said, 'So let's hear the worst.'

'It's simple,' Rossi told him. 'Your record in the field of international intelligence makes you a very valuable commodity. Of course, I could simply shoot you, but that would be a waste. What I get for you will in some way make up for the financial loss over the *Mona Lisa* debacle.'

'There's only one problem with that,' Ferguson said cheerfully. 'My value would depend on what I had to say, and I'm not a very talkative individual.'

'Oh, we can take care of that. A little drug called Succinylcholine. It's used as a muscle relaxant in certain operations, but only if the patient is unconscious. If he isn't, it leaves him totally paralysed, unable to breathe and in exquisite pain. The effect lasts two minutes, but the idea of a repeat performance would be too terrible to contemplate. No, you'd sing for your supper.'

And Ferguson knew fear as he never had before, but managed a smile. 'Sounds pretty ghastly,' and he turned to the Baron. 'And you would approve of this business?'

'I'm sure I won't have to. You will, of course, be sensible.'

* * *

Halfway up the great stone stairs was a small viewing room to one side, a very medieval item with an open front through which one could see everything in the Great Hall. Dillon, Billy and Klein, staying cautiously back, had a clear enough sight.

The magnificent chandelier hanging from the boarded ceiling illuminated the scene below: the oak table; the silver candlesticks, candles flaring; Newton and Cook on the landing at the top of the marble stairs; Gibson by the log fire; the Baron and Ferguson seated opposite each other; Rossi to one side.

Dillon took it all in and pulled them back. 'Does this staircase link up to the other landing?' he asked Klein in German.

'Yes.'

'And the door down below is the only way into the Great Hall?'

'That's right.'

'Good. I'll send my friend up to the landing and I'll go through the door.'

'And what about me?'

'You stay here and keep watch.'

'Now, look . . .'

Dillon said, 'Do as you're told.' He jammed his machine pistol against Klein's chest. 'I mean it.'

Klein put up a hand. 'Okay – fine.'

Billy said, 'Is he being awkward?'

'More like a pain in the arse. Go up those stairs, turn at the top and you'll be on the landing overlooking the Hall. Think you can handle Newton and Cook?'

'Any day, including my day off. What about you?'

'I'll go downstairs and go in hard through the Hall door. Fifty, Billy, counting from now.' They parted, Billy up and Dillon down. Klein, furious, took out the bottle of schnapps and drank from it, then went back into the viewing room, taking out his sawn-off shotgun.

Below, Rossi was saying, 'I thought an auction might be fun.'

'You do like to twist the knife, old son,' Ferguson said. 'Like the ivory Madonna. Oh, I know all about that. When you were on the run behind Serb lines, you killed four people, only two of whom were women. You make a habit of that. Witness Sara Hesser.'

'Damn you, Ferguson,' Rossi cried, his right hand coming out of his pocket holding the Madonna.

At the same moment, Klein, up above and thoroughly drunk, leaned out and shouted, 'I've got you now, Baron,' hurled the empty schnapps bottle and fired both barrels of his sawn-off.

Strangely enough, it was Ferguson who saved the Baron, hurling himself forward and knocking him from his chair, but it was Derry Gibson, the old Irish hand, who got Klein, firing a Browning three times, catching Klein in the forehead, sending him back into the wall to bounce over the edge and fall into the Hall below.

All of their timing was blown. Billy, advancing on Newton and Cook, had no choice but to shoot Newton while Dillon, below, kicked in the door, stood to one side and sprayed across.

Ferguson and the Baron were behind the sofa, Rossi and Gibson upended the table and fired towards the door.

Dillon called, 'You okay, Billy?'

'Got Newton, Cook to go.'

There was a burst of firing. Dillon called, 'See what you can do with the chandelier. I'll help. One, two, three, go.'

They gave it sustained fire, it splintered, shards flying everywhere, sagged, then ripped out of the ceiling, plunging the Hall into darkness, and crashed to the floor, parts of it showering the table.

On the landing, Cook panicked totally and stood up firing his AK47. Billy drove him back with a short burst, then started down the stairs. Dillon ran in, firing high, and confronted Rossi and Derry Gibson as they emerged from behind the wreck of the chandelier and table. Billy came up behind them.

'Hold it.' He ran his hands over them, and relieved them of two pistols and Rossi of the ivory Madonna. He sprang the blade. 'That's handy.' He snapped the blade shut and put it in his pocket.

Ferguson and the Baron were standing now. Ferguson said, 'What kept you?'

Billy said, 'From what I could see from up there, you saved this old sod. What on earth for?'

'It seemed like the civilized thing to do, and he was very civilized to me, Dillon. He took me to the chapel and produced a tantalizing glimpse of the diary. Hidden in the mausoleum.'

'Really? Well, we came for you, Charles, but the diary is definitely a bonus.'

Rossi hadn't said a word, merely stood there glowering, and Gibson was poised to take any chance to run for it, Dillon knew that.

'All right,' he said to Rossi. 'Lead the way.'

Coming in at six hundred feet, Kubel had a perfect view of the Schloss, wonderfully floodlit, the meadow below. At one hundred and sixty miles per hour, he'd made a quick run in spite of the heavy rain, but at the end, it had faded into a drizzle. There was a quarter-moon, pale, rain-washed, and then the floodlit Schloss, the great meadow, and he went down and made a perfect landing, taxied to the far end, turned and taxied back. His Codex Four sounded and he replied.

'Kubel.'

'Dillon here. Heard you coming in. We've got him.'

'Fine. Ready to leave when you are.'

* * *

They grouped close to the mausoleum in the chapel, Billy covering Rossi, Gibson and the Baron with his Schmeisser. Ferguson fiddled about at the back.

'It's in here somewhere, a secret cavity of some sort.'

'You'll never find it,' the Baron said tranquilly.

'I haven't got time to waste.' Dillon grabbed Rossi by the hair, took a Walther from the pocket of his raincoat and rammed the muzzle against the side of the skull. 'Produce it or I'll kill him.'

'I don't think so.'

'Then you don't know me.' Dillon turned to Gibson. 'I told you never to run back to me.' He shot him between the eyes, hurling him back against the steps of the mausoleum, blood flying.

There was general shock, and then he rammed the muzzle of the Walther against Rossi's skull again.

'It's up to you.'

'No,' the Baron cried in anguish. 'I'll give it to you, but only if you swear on your honour to spare him.'

It was Ferguson who intervened. 'You have my word.'

The old man went to the back of the mausoleum, and there was one slight creaking as he opened the cavity. He came back with the diary and held it out to Ferguson, who took it.

'A "holy book", according to Sara Hesser. You swore an oath never to copy it.'

'I never did.'

'Excellent.' Ferguson went up the two steps to the eternal flame and dropped the diary inside. It started to burn at once.

Rossi cried out, 'You bloody fool, Father, they'll kill us anyway.'

Dillon shoved him away and raised his Walther, but Ferguson said, 'No, it's over, and I did give my word. We leave now,' and he walked out.

'You're a lucky man,' Dillon said. 'I gave up on honour a long time ago. Come on, Billy.' They went out, following

Ferguson back along the tunnel, hurrying past the carnage in the Great Hall and out to the front door, turning down the steps to the courtyard. Several vehicles were parked there, including a Land Rover with the keys in it.

'This will do,' Dillon said, and got behind the wheel. The other two scrambled in and he drove away and out across the drawbridge.

Rossi emerged from the front of the chapel, his father on his heels, and looked far down into the meadow. 'My God, it's a Storch, they're leaving in an old crate like that. Well, I'll show them.'

He stormed down the path to the courtyard, and his father stumbled along behind him. 'But what are you going to do?'

'My Gulfstream is three times faster than that thing. I'll run the bastards into the ground.'

He was beside himself with rage.

'You're crazy,' the Baron said, as he plucked at Rossi's sleeve. Rossi pulled away, started to run, and the old man went after him.

In the courtyard, Rossi scrambled into a station wagon, switched it on, drove for the gate and found the Baron standing there, arms outstretched, the familiar cane in one hand. Rossi had no option but to stop, and the Baron had the passenger door open in a second and hauled himself in.

'Whatever we do, we do together. Now get on with it.'

Ferguson, Dillon and Billy packed into the Storch, and Max Kubel grinned and shouted over the roaring of the engine, 'All's well that ends well. Let's get the hell out of here.'

'A sound idea. We've left four dead men up there,' Ferguson told him.

'Then we really had better get moving.' He boosted power, roared down the meadow and lifted into the air.

Dillon looked out and down in time to see the station wagon drawing up to the Gulfstream, and gestured. Kubel glanced back.

'If you didn't leave Rossi dead back there, then that will be him. There's no one else it could be. Let's move it.'

He didn't have a hope, of course; there was no way of getting away, not with the Gulfstream's speed. There was no chance of being shot down, because the Gulfstream wasn't a fighting aircraft, which meant only one thing. He was going to get bounced. Rossi would force him to crash in the forest, and Rossi was a damn good pilot.

He was at one thousand feet when he felt a great shock wave. The Storch rocked in the turbulence; the Gulfstream passed over them, then banked, came around and took up a station to port as Rossi reduced speed. He had the cockpit lights on and, looking across, Dillon could see von Berger sitting in the right-hand pilot's seat, staring out.

'My god, he's got the Baron with him,' he shouted. The Gulfstream roared away, banked and came back towards them head-on, lifting at the last moment and passing over, the Storch rocking again in the turbulence.

'No,' Kubel thought. 'He's trying to force me down so low I'll hit the trees. Let's play a different game.'

He hauled back the column and climbed to two-and-a-half thousand feet, and in the cockpit of the Gulfstream, Rossi snarled, 'What in the hell is he doing, that pilot?'

'This is ridiculous,' the Baron said. 'Madness. Let's go back.'

'I'm damned if I will.'

And at that moment, Kubel took the Storch nose-down into the steepest dive of his career, and Rossi went roaring after him. The Storch held true and Kubel didn't haul back the column until the last suicidal moment, levelling at five hundred feet.

The Baron placed his hand over Rossi's. 'It's enough,' he said, and pushed the control column forward. The Gulfstream, chasing at four hundred miles an hour, ploughed straight into the forest in a ball of fire.

Dillon shouted to Kubel, 'You're a genius.'

'He wasn't in his right mind,' Kubel replied. 'Nobody flying a plane that way could be.'

'It was his choice,' Ferguson said. 'I can't say I'm sorry. He had a terrible fate in mind for me, and the Baron was going to stand by and let him get on with it.'

'They can roast in hell as far as I'm concerned,' Dillon said. 'Let's go home.'

They came into Arnheim shortly afterwards and landed by the hangar, where Hannah, Harry, Lacey and Perry waited.

'My God, it's great to see you, General,' Harry said.

Hannah impulsively kissed Ferguson on the cheek. 'I'm so glad you made it, sir.'

'Well, all that can wait. All aboard. I want us out of here fast. Dillon, you and Billy had better change. What about you?' Ferguson asked Kubel.

'Oh, I'll fly off after you're gone. Time for an extended holiday, I think.'

'You were wonderful back there.'

'Yes, I was, wasn't I?'

Lacey and Parry were in the cockpit of the Citation, Hannah and Harry boarded, Ferguson followed and Dillon and Billy came running out of the hangar a moment later.

Dillon said to Kubel, 'I thought I was a good pilot, but you're a great pilot. Isn't he a great pilot, Billy?'

'Bleeding marvellous. Let's go.'

They went up the Airstair door and Parry closed it behind them. A few moments later, they were rolling down the runway, taking off and climbing fast.

'Okay, what happened?' Harry demanded.

'It can wait, Harry,' Ferguson said. 'As usual, they covered themselves with glory.' He turned to Hannah. 'Be kind enough to call Roper. Mission accomplished, Hitler diary destroyed. Baron Max von Berger, Marco Rossi and Derry Gibson departed this life for who knows what? Ask him to relay that information to Blake Johnson, too.'

'Of course, sir, and the Prime Minister?'

'I'll deal with him myself.'

She went to the back of the cabin and moved into the kitchen for privacy. Harry got the bar cupboard open. 'I reckon a drink's in order, except for Billy here.'

'I'm going to have a kip anyway,' Billy said, putting his seat back and closing his eyes.

'Bushmills.' Harry held the bottle up. 'You've got friends at court, you little Irish sod.'

He found three glasses and paused. There was a kind of companionable silence. They drank it down and Harry poured again.

Ferguson toasted Dillon, 'A hard one, Sean, but you did well.'

'They get harder,' Dillon said. 'I sometimes think I should find a better class of work.'

Ferguson shook his head and said softly, 'Don't be silly. Where on earth would you go?'